John Davenport

An Account of the Observance of the one Hundred and

Fiftieth

Anniversary of the Organization of the Congregational Church....

John Davenport

An Account of the Observance of the one Hundred and Fiftieth
Anniversary of the Organization of the Congregational Church....

ISBN/EAN: 9783744764216

Printed in Europe, USA, Canada, Australia, Japan

Cover: Foto ©Andreas Hilbeck / pixelio.de

More available books at **www.hansebooks.com**

1726. 1876.

AN ACCOUNT OF THE OBSERVANCE OF THE

ONE HUNDRED AND FIFTIETH ANNIVERSARY

OF THE

ORGANIZATION

OF THE

Congregational Church,

WILTON, CONN., JUNE 22, 1876,

INCLUDING A

HISTORICAL ADDRESS,

By SAMUEL G. WILLARD,

AND

A POEM,

By JOHN G. DAVENPORT.

NEW YORK :
R. J. Johnston, Printer, 181 William St.
1876.

INTRODUCTION.

At the Annual Meeting of the WILTON CONGREGATIONAL CHURCH, held January 7th, 1876, the Pastor, Deacons and Standing Committee were authorized to make arrangements for an appropriate celebration of the One Hundred and Fiftieth Anniversary of the Organization of this Church in the month of June following.

At the first meeting of the Committee, Rev. SAMUEL G. WILLARD, of Colchester, was invited to prepare an Address for the occasion and Rev. JOHN G. DAVENPORT, of Bridgeport, a Poem. At this meeting the Committee voted to add to their number the Society's Committee.

After repeated meetings the following invitation and order of exercises was prepared and sent (so far as their address could be obtained) to all *natives* of the town holding former relations to this Church and Society :

1726. 1876.

ONE HUNDRED AND FIFTIETH ANNIVERSARY

OF THE

WILTON CONGREGATIONAL CHURCH
AND SOCIETY,

THURSDAY, JUNE 22d, 1876.

You are respectfully invited to meet with the friends of this Church and Society, on Thursday, June 22d, at half-past 10, A. M., and share in the privileges of the occasion.

Hon. CHARLES JONES, of New York, has been invited to act as President of the day.

The Address of Welcome will be given by Rev. S. J. M. MERWIN, Pastor.

Response by Rev. JAMES W. HUBBELL, of New Haven.

Historical Address by Rev. S. G. WILLARD, of Colchester.

Poem by Rev. J. G. DAVENPORT, of Bridgeport.

The Ladies will provide a Collation, to be served after the close of the exercises in the church.

Please reply to

REV. S. J. M. MERWIN, OR EDWARD OLMSTEAD.

Rev. H. N. DUNNING and Rev. D. R. AUSTIN, of South Norwalk, with Rev. Dr. N. BOUTON, of Concord, N. H., conducted the devotional exercises, and the Choir of the Church, led by Mr. R. J. JOHNSTON, chorister, furnished the music for the occasion. Mr. FRANK COMSTOCK presided at the Organ.

After the Collation the Church was again filled, and the remainder of the day spent in listening to addresses from Rev. E. MIX, of Orange, N. J., Rev. Dr. NATHANIEL BOUTON, of Concord, N. H., Rev. H. N. DUNNING, of South Norwalk, EUGENE SMITH, Esq., and C. L. WESTCOTT, Esq., of New York, and others.

The meeting was closed with singing "Hold the Fort."

By vote, the Historical Address, Poem, and other Addresses of the morning were ordered to be printed.

Rev. S. J. M. MERWIN,   } *Publication*
Dea. EDWARD OLMSTEAD, } *Committee.*

Wilton, Conn., July 29th, **1876.**

PROCEEDINGS.

THE exercises were commenced by the Pastor, the Rev. S. J. M. MERWIN, calling upon CHARLES JONES, Esq., of New York, to occupy the Chair. He was received with a hearty welcome. Mr. JONES said—

LADIES AND GENTLEMEN: I thank you for this cordial greeting. I confess that it was with some reluctance that I accepted the invitation of your Committee to preside on this occasion, because I thought, as I doubt not many of you now think, that the place would be better filled by a perma-nent resident of the town and one sustaining official relations to the Church and congregation; but still I do not feel that I am an alien or a stranger here. None of you have a stronger or a warmer affection for this good old town than I have. And pleasant and agreable as are my associations in the city where I live (the City of Brooklyn) and where so many of the men and women of New England take up their resi-dence, no school-boy so longs for his vacation as I long for the return of Summer, when I can come home again to the rest which I always find in this quiet place—the place I know and love so well. Its hills and its valleys, its woods and its cultivated fields, its meadows and its orchards, its running brooks, its byways and highways—I know them all so well and so intimately that they have come to form a part of my very self. So, ladies and gentlemen, I feel that by nativity, in heart, mind, and in my whole being, I am a Wiltonian, and it gives me pleasure to join with you in the exercises of this day.

We have come up here, on this bright and beautiful Summer morning, with loving hearts, to record our homage for the Christian men and women who, one hundred and fifty years ago, planted here a Church—a Church which to-day is older by a half century than the nation. And it is good for us to be here as children. "Honor thy father and thy mother" is the Divine command, and, during all the centuries since it was delivered from the smoking mount to man, it has always found an echo in the heart of every loving, dutiful child. And we are especially bound—we, the sons and daughters of New England, are called upon by every sentiment of affection, of gratitude, of reverence, aye, of pride, even—to honor and hold in remembrance the heroic men and women who planted on the soil of New England the Free Church, from which have sprung a Free State and a Free Nation!

My friends, we do take pride, and we justly take pride, in our ancestry. For have we not seen the great work which they did, all unconsciously to themselves, and how worldwide has been its influence? Yes, my friends, as clearly as you can track the course of an overflowing river through an arid waste by the verdure on its banks, just as clearly can you trace the stream of New England civilization in its flow from ocean to ocean across the continent, bearing with it whatever is best and whatever is noblest in our social, our educational and our religious life, the family with its purity, the free school and the academy with their faithful teachers, the college and the university with their learned professors, and above all, and greatest of all, the Church with its messengers of peace and love.

Ladies and gentlemen, the pilgrim spirit is not dead—no, the pilgrim spirit is not dead. "It walks in the moon's broad light, and it watches by the bed of the glorious dead with the holy stars at night." And if it so be that by the commemoration services of this day we shall catch somewhat more of that spirit and carry it with us from this place, it will not be in vain that we have met here to do honor to the little band of Christian men and women who planted here a Church which has been a source of comfort and blessing to the generations that have come and gone during the one hundred and fifty years of its existence. (Applause.)

An Anthem—"Jehovah's Praise"—was then sung by the Choir; the Solo being sung by Mrs. SAMUEL MARVIN, daughter of the Chorister.

The Rev. Mr. H. N. DUNNING, of South Norwalk, read the 145th Psalm.

The CHAIRMAN—Rev. Mr. MERWIN will extend a Welcome to the Wiltonian pilgrims who have come up here to day.

REMARKS OF REV. MR. MERWIN.

THIS pleasant duty has been devolved upon me by the Committee, and, as I told the brother who is to follow me, I suppose all I have to say is, "We are very glad to see you." But he says if I stop there all he shall say will be " Thank you—very much obliged." So I suppose I must go on a little further; and indeed it is in my heart to express to you our most sincere pleasure at seeing so many of you here on this occasion; that the Lord has favored us with such beautiful weather, and that so many of you have left your household cares and your domestic duties, your farms and your merchandise, your offices and your school-rooms, and your various occupations, and come up to help us celebrate this One Hundred and Fiftieth Anniversary of the Organization of our Church. And we feel that we ought to extend a special welcome to all of you who have ever been connected with this Church, and that covers more ground, perhaps, than you suppose. Not only do we welcome those of you who were baptized in this Church, and those of you who here came forward and publicly professed your faith in the Lord Jesus Christ, and those of you who brought letters from other Churches and thus united with this Church of Christ, but also all whose parents or grandparents or great-grandparents were ever connected with this Church; and this, as I said, perhaps covers more ground than you suppose—for one hundred and fifty

years ago all persons were required by law to attend
Church on Sundays, Fast Days and Thanksgiving, under
penalty of a fine of five shillings for every absence; and
therefore it is to be presumed that one hundred and fifty
years ago all the people went to Church. And for
more than fifty years this was the only Church here
in Wilton, so that those of you who have ever lived in Wilton, or have come down from the old Wilton families are
more or less connected with this old Wilton Church; and the
mother to-day hails you all as her children, even though
some of you may have wandered away into the Methodist
woods, or gone down into the deep waters of the Baptist per-
suasion, or taken refuge in the Episcopal fold. We hail you
all as common children of this mother Church, and as re-
joicing in the prosperity of the kingdom of our Lord and
Saviour Jesus Christ.

And we welcome you back to these old hills and these
fields where, in early days, you gathered wild flowers and
strawberries, and to these old school-houses where you sat
down on the hard slab-seats and carved your names to Yan-
kee immortality, and to this Church of Christ where you
came, some of you, perhaps, sitting in the gallery seats and
leaving on the walls a record which you hoped might be un-
dying—but the whitewasher's brush has wiped it off long ere
this.

To-day, let the lawyer forget his clients, and the judge his
court, and the doctor his patients (perhaps they will be all
the better for it), and the teacher his pupils, and the ladies
their domestic cares (at least those of you who have come from
abroad). We want you all to be boys and girls again, and
bring up the memories of old times, especially after you have
gone out from these walls and are gathered together on this
old Green, where so many of you played ball when you
were boys.

For some two or three hours, perhaps, we will stay in
school and listen to our masters, and learn well the lessons
they have to teach us, and then—you know how there never
was a time when we had such wild delight and joyous glee

as when school was out and we rushed out of doors. So, when we have listened here for a while, we shall be all the more ready to participate in the festivities of the occasion.

The CHAIRMAN—The Rev. JAMES W. HUBBELL, a native of Wilton, but now a resident of New Haven, will respond to the Address of Welcome.

REMARKS OF REV. MR. HUBBELL.

OUR friend here, in his very kind welcome, has gone so far beyond the short address he had thought to give us, that if to that, I should have had nothing to say but "thank you," now after all he has so well said, I do not feel equal to the occasion. Especially when I find, Mr. Chairman, that over and above all that he has said, we had been so beautifully and profusely welcomed by the flowers in the vestibule, by this old sanctuary putting on to-day such a glad and welcome attire, by all these faces so dear and familiar, whose every radiant feature has spoken welcome.

Why, sir, these many-toned welcomes have made us feel at home again, as though we had not really lost our inheritance here; that we are not aliens or strangers—but have a fellowship with these Saints and with this Household of God. It is said that the sons of old England, wherever they roam, carry home with them, and though exiled and expatriated they belong to old England still. So it is, sir, with some of us who find ourselves coming back here with no home to visit; the old places in the possession of strangers; no rights here in property; the families scattered, yet this dear old town still is and ever will be our home.

It is good to come up to Zion on this anniversary day to recall the scenes of the past; to recall the faces and the names that had almost faded from memory; to recall the history of this old and honored Church, of its pastors, of its deacons, of its members. It is good for each of us to come back to the beginning of things; to trace back the roots of our lives to their sources and to find them fed from deep and hidden springs among these hills. It is good for us to see what influences helped shape us and to ask whether we have been faithful to our early teachings and vows.

Thomas Arnold of Rugby has said that when boys have graduated from school, and have passed on into earnest life, that however much they may have been neglected or abused, however distasteful their school life may have been at the time of it, they will love to revisit the scenes of their youth, and they will remember with only gratitude all that was done for them. So does it seem to us all; out of whatever divergent paths we come back to this one place where we were wont to meet on Sabbath days. This place to which, perhaps, some of us did not come so willingly and so thankfully as we come this morning.

And, oh, what a charm memory has, to touch with her magic wand scenes long past, and make them present once more—to touch the graves on yonder hill side, and make them give up their dead, to lead them in long procession, so that they shall walk these aisles once more, and sit here before us in their old places, with their old familiar look. to sing and pray, and listen and sleep, as they used to do in those far off days. What a power has memory that she can touch this comely sanctuary as it is to-day with its new-fangled fresco and organ, with its modern pulpit and pews, and convert them into that old meeting-house of five and thirty years ago, so dear and familiar to some of us, with its plain walls and lofty pulpit, with its majestic sounding-board above it, and the square, straight-back pews, and the lofty galleries with that tremendous choir, fiddle, base-viol and all!

I say for myself (and I am sure I am uttering the sentiments of all these boys and girls, young and old, who have returned here that they might join in these festivities), if we have reaped any success in life, if at the bar or in the pulpit, if as teachers, if as men of business and cares, we have been or are being useful in our generation, it is one of the greatest pleasures we have, to claim this dear old town as our native place, and this Church, where our fathers worshipped, as the hallowed spot where those good men that are gone sprinkled us in holy baptism and taught us in the way of life, where we had our first thoughts of God and of eternity, where many of us, in the enthusiasm of early youth, consecrated ourselves to God and our generation.

It is with feelings of pride, pardonable on this memorial day, that we recall the honorable names of both living and dead, of both men and women, who have gone from this Church. More than a score of them have passed, and some of them with high honors, through collegiate and professional study; one of them has a name conspicuous not only in our own land and in this century, but conspicuous throughout all lands where the Bible is studied. I am reminded here of an incident of this distinguished scholar, Professor Moses Stuart, told me recently by one who heard it, that after preaching in this Church two or three Sabbaths during a vacation, as he often did to the delight of the people, the Pastor said, just before his sermon on the following Sabbath: "My dear people, you have had one of your distinguished sons to preach, for a few times, most remarkable sermons; you must now be content to put up with more common fare." And I would not forget the many distinguished men who were here in preparatory study; some of them we are glad to see present to-day, who were earnest helpers in this Church, and whose memories are yet fragrant.

But I must not continue these thoughts, but leave them for others who are to follow me. Allow me to say in closing, that this day is one of peculiar joy to us boys and girls who return here, and we wish to thank you all for your very kind greetings. But to some of us there are sad thoughts as we return to find voices that welcomed in the past, now hushed in death, and hands that used to grasp ours in welcome, now forever still. We find strangers living where we used to dwell; only let us resolve as we go hence, that we will teach our children the principles that were taught us, and that we will train them, as we were trained, for usefulness on earth and for happiness in heaven; so that the lives of those who have gone before will be perpetuated in the generations that are to follow.

I would close with the following sentiment: This day of

June, auspiciously one of the longest of the year, with a profusion of flowers and evergreens; may it be to this Church the symbol and the prophecy of a long day of un-fading beauty and blessedness—the beauty of holiness—the blessedness of usefulness; and when it at last closes, to close only to open into the brightness of the eternal morning, where gladder bells shall usher in the day.

The following Hymn, composed for the occasion by Miss ELIZABETH STUART PHELPS, granddaughter of Prof. Moses Stuart, a native of Wilton, was then sung by the Choir:

God of the centuries! who art
The Home of every homeless heart,
The Wisdom to our foolishness,
The Rest of all our weariness.

We are too dull to understand
The gentle pressure of Thy hand;
Too blind to see (or cold to try)
The light of love within Thine eye.

Lost children in the mystery
That darkens 'twixt our souls and Thee,
We join our trembling hands and cry,
"Show Thyself to us, or we die!"

In the dim thicket called Thy Church
We grope for Thee—O! to our search
Be growing Light.   While weak we roam,
Be Strength, be Hope, be Love, be Home.

We bless the gloom in which Thou art,
We hear the beatings of Thy heart—
Across the shadow tortuous,
Oh, God! we know it beats for us.

O! clasp us to it!—hold us there!
Till some glad day the dawn breaks fair,
Till on the sweet far plains it fall,
And Truth for one is Truth for all.

The CHAIRMAN—We have reached the point of chief interest in our Anniversary proceedings. The Historical Address will now be delivered by a gentleman born in this town, taught in its schools, and early connected with this Church—the Rev. SAMUEL G. WILLARD. Although he, at the present time, ministers to a people in a remote part of the State (Colchester), yet neither distance nor absence has weakened his affection for this place and this Church.

HISTORICAL ADDRESS.

THE words of the Psalmist that may fitly introduce the outline of a History of this Church, which its Committee have invited me to prepare for this the One Hundred and Fiftieth Anniversary of its Organization, may be found in the first verse of the forty-fourth Psalm :

" WE HAVE HEARD WITH OUR EARS, O GOD !
  OUR FATHERS HAVE TOLD US,
  WHAT WORK THOU DIDST IN THEIR DAYS,
  IN THE TIMES OF OLD."—*Psalm* 44: 1.

The hopeful face of youth is towards the future, the eye of age scans pensively the past. Youth sees in mementoes of departed years gray hairs, wrinkles, decrepitude, and the gloom of the grave, while the days to come are spanned by the bow of promise, and scarcely darkened save by the shadows of coming achievements. Age sees in the same direction dubious pleasures, and certain sorrow; but in the past, treasures of experience and of wisdom; worthy to be diligently sought out.

To the young the reminiscences of their grandparents are often without interest. But in later life, they may vainly regret the lost opportunity to learn from lips which death long ago sealed.

The people of New England, in the vigorous youth of the nation, were for two centuries or more so intensely occupied with the difficulties of laying the foundations of government, and in maintaining liberty, civil and religious, that they had scanty opportunity to record their deeds. But in the last

generation, a desire to know who and what those brave and
wise men were, has stimulated a search among the memo-
rials of their lives, which time has spared.

The anniversary of a settlement of a town, or of the organization of a church, has been made the occasion to revive, for
the satisfaction of the living and the instruction of those that
may succeed them, the worthy deeds of the founders and of
their successors.

Twenty-five years ago, the Two Hundredth Anniversary
of the settlement of Norwalk, of which Wilton was for above
one hundred and fifty years a part, was duly celebrated, and
a Historical Discourse delivered, by Rev. Nathaniel Bouton,
D.D., of Concord, New Hampshire, who was a native of Norwalk, and who, by his presence, honors this occasion. Four
years earlier, Rev. Edwin Hall, D.D., then pastor of the
First Church in Norwalk, and now Emeritus Professor of
Theology in the Seminary at Auburn, N. Y., had laid the
people of Norwalk and vicinity under lasting obligations, by
diligently copying out and publishing, town, society and other
ancient records.

Seventy-five years younger than the honored mother, this
Church, to-day, in the maturity of her powers, but without a
gray lock or a furrow of care, glowing with youth and beauty
whch we fondly believe may be immortal, calls her children to rejoice with her, that the Heavenly Father has brought
her prosperously to the end of the third half century of her
existence.

As the parish was for three-quarters of a century in its
boundaries nearly identical with the town that now is, a full
history of the Church for that period would include a history
of the town. But as this is the Anniversary of the organization of the Church and not of the Town, much that would
belong to a history of the latter, must needs be omitted.

The period under review is, in one aspect, not long ; for
there are those now members of the Church whose grandparents were living at its beginning. Possibly there may be
some here, who have spoken with one or more individuals
who were living at that time.

And yet the materials for a history of this sort, so far as known, are not abundant. The pious care of the second minister, and of some of his successors in office, the more or less imperfect records of the Ecclesiastical Society, are the chief, direct and original contributions to this history in the possession of the Church and Society. From the records of Norwalk, from old account books, letters and manuscripts hid away in old attics, much, no doubt, might be gleaned. And there should be letters in the hands of descendants of Wilton families, whose residence is in some other place, letters dating, some of them at least, a hundred years back, which would furnish most interesting information. Mr. Philip Betts made, nearly twenty years since, an abstract of the Society records and of a portion of the Church records, which I have been permitted to consult in the preparation of this discourse. The original records—except notes from the earlier portion, made sixteen or seventeen years since in summer vacations—have not been in my reach during the short interval allowed · for the work.

At the outset, a brief notice of the settlement of this town may claim attention.

From the time of the founding of New Haven in 1638 until 1690, most of the towns organized, in what is now Connecticut, unless near Hartford, were on the shore of the sound. As the inhabitants increased, the disposition to emigrate, which continues to this day, was seen. After the death of Philip (in 1676) released the people from the fear of Indian violence, they began to push northward. Between 1690 and 1725, a considerable number of townships were formed adjoining the shore towns on the north. Some time during this period, lands were taken up and houses built in what is now Wilton. Tradition says that the house in Norwalk, near the Wilton line, known as the Odell place, was built over two hundred years ago by a Mr. Whitney, and that a house in Cranberry Plain built by a Mr. Gregory is somewhat older. The first house south of the Kent school-house is reported to be about as old.* Another tradition has it, that the house

* Charles M. Gregory, Norwalk.

north of the school-house, across the street, formerly occupied by Rev. Mr. Gaylord, was raised on the same day. These traditions may be accepted for what they are worth. In 1685, eight families, all from Norwalk, save one from Stratford, began the settlement of Danbury, and in 1708 a company of Norwalk men purchased land and began to settle Ridgefield. A committee was appointed in 1713 to lay out a highway from Norwalk thither. In 1725 the inhabitants in Kent, Belden's Hill and Chestnut were sufficiently numerous to ask to be made a separate parish. It is therefore highly probable that houses began to be built in Wilton at least as early as in Ridgefield, and probably as early as 1701. The style of building is seen in the houses already named. A common, not invariable, fashion, was the two story front, the second story in some cases projecting beyond the first; the rear roof extending within six feet of the ground; the large stone chimney in the center with its wide fire-place, the house set without regard to the road, so as to indicate the four points of the compass, the door nearest the street midway between the ends of the house, window frames hardly more than twenty-eight by forty inches, and window glass seven inches by nine, the whole undisguised by paint out of doors or in.

The first public movement to form a separate parish was December 7, 1725, when the town of Norwalk which was then co-terminous with the Ecclesiastical Society: "by a major vote, signified their willingness that the inhabitants of Kent, Belden's Hill and Chestnut Hill, and so upwards, become a parish or village by themselves." At the same meeting a committee was appointed "to joyne with a committee from ye said inhabitants, in viewing where ye bounds may be best fixt for ye said upper village, and make a report to ye town of their opinion." The little brook at the lower end of Kent formed a convenient starting point from which the committees proceeded east and west, and fixed the bounds substantially where the present bounds of the town are, the eastern boundary excepted.

This period was an era in the history of Norwalk. A new town house or the enlargement of the school-house for town meetings must be made; town meetings must no longer be held in the house of worship; a number of persons are peacefully allowed to draw off to the Church of England,"* and at the same time—there was serious difficulty on account of the minister, Rev. Stephen Buckingham, by reason of some irregularities in his conduct (the temperance reformation had not then begun), which difficulties perhaps hastened the formation of the Episcopal Society. An Ecclesiastical Council was called to give advice. In the end Mr. Buckingham resigned and Rev. Moses Dickinson was installed in 1727. †

There were thirty-one petitioners to the General Assembly in Hartford, that the parish might be constituted. Most of the names are, or were within the memory of persons now living, still found in this town. The Act of incorporation was passed May 12th, 1726. So far as I know, the name Wilton, so euphonious and often admired by its people, first appears—in this connection—in the petition to the General Assembly, and was adopted by that body. Whence the name came, we can only conjecture. When the genealogical register of each of the families of the petitioners shall have been made, it may be found that one or more of them was descended from a family in Wilton, Wiltshire, England, a place of much importance even eleven hundred years ago. ‡

The Prime Ancient Society of Norwalk was disposed to deal generously with the new parish. February 28th, 1726, it voted "to the inhabitants of ye upper Society, the old pulpit upon free gift," and the next February it voted that the Proprietors in Norwalk grant them ten acres of land for "the use of ye Presbyterian or Congregational Ministry among them forever." Two years later five acres more were given. The harmony thus early existing between the two parishes has happily continued to this day.

---

* Prof. Kingsley, of Yale College, says that at this time there were in Connecticut only two or three congregations of Episcopalians, and two of Baptists, all small; no congregation of Quakers.—Hall's Norwalk, p. 157.

† Webster's History of Presbyterian Church, p. 373, says the call was voted August 19th, and the parish of Wilton concurred in the call the next day.

‡ The foundation of its famous Abbey was begun in 773.

Whether, however, this Ecclesiastical Society was faithful to its trust, when, in 1754, it sold nine acres of this parsonage land to Benjamin Betts for £155 14s., old tenor, and, so far as appears, used the money for current expenses, is a question.

In family affairs, sometimes the bride is first obtained, and she helps to plan and build the house. In the Christian economy, naturally the Church comes first, then the Society (if it is necessary to have a Society), and the house of worship last, builded by the Church and Society. In this case the Society was first, the arrangements for the Church edifice seem to have come next, the selection of a Pastor followed, and the organization of the Church—the most important step of all —came after these.

It is much to be regretted that there is no account of this transaction. The Society records show a meeting (the second, or rather an adjourned meeting of that body) on the 12th of June, which confirmed the doings of the meeting of June 7th, and appointed a committee to make arrangements with some of the neighboring Pastors, for organizing a Church and securing the settlement of Mr. Sturgeon. They voted to request two of the near neighboring Pastors "to attend and assist in carrying on a day of fasting and prayer amongst them, to look to God for guidance and direction in the affairs before them, and in a due and suitable time to obtain the settling of the said Mr. Sturgeon." At the same time Jonathan Elmer* was chosen "to read the Psalm and John St. John to set the tune to the Psalm at all times usual in the public worship." As we hear no more of the organization of the Church, but find it apparently organized on the 27th of June, though it is not mentioned by name, we may conjecture that event to have occurred between the Society's meeting of June 14th and June 27th, and on that day of fasting and prayer in which the two "near neighboring Pastors," according to invitation, were present. The Manual of this Church, printed A. D. 1857, says it was organized "about the 20th of June." But as the

---

* The Elmers seem to have been earlier in Fairfield. Jonathan Elmer, Yale College, 1747, was ordained Pastor, New Providence, New Jersey, 1750, and remained 43 years ; he died June 7, 1807. —Webster, page 608.

20th of June that year was Monday, and therefore a less convenient day than Wednesday, the 22d, we may perhaps be
permitted to assume that on this latter day, just one hundred
and fifty years ago, this Church began to be. As the Saybrook Platform and Confession was then eighteen years old,
and fully accepted by the neighboring Churches, we may suppose that the form of organization and the creed of the Church
were easily arranged.

The difficulty of procuring a Pastor, as already stated, was
soon overcome. June 7th the Society elected Richard
Bouton, clerk, and voted unanimously to call Rev. ROBERT
STURGEON to officiate in the work of the ministry amongst
them, and fixed his salary at "ninety pounds, paramount or
equivalent to good bills of credit of the Colony of Connecticut, or other good bills of credit, passing current at the re-
spective times of payment," and "a full supply of firewood for
his family's use," * * "to be brought to his habitation from
time to time as is needed." Five acres of land were also granted for a " house lot."

Mr. Sturgeon had not been long in this country, and probably reached Wilton in April, as his salary commenced the
14th of that month. He was of Scotch, or probably of Scotch-
Irish, descent. After completing his studies in his own country,
the Presbytery, for some reason, declined to give him a license
to preach. On reaching New England, he was approbated by
a Council, says a Presbyterian writer,* "greatly to the regret
of Cotton Mather, who believed that his conduct had justified
the Presbytery in refusing a license." When or by whom he
was ordained is not clear. In the Society's record he is called
Reverend, and is said to have been installed. But an Association must license before a Council could ordain. Who would
call a Council to ordain a comparative stranger as an evangelist,
in those days when ordination and installation almost always
went together, is not apparent. Much to our regret, there is
no Church record prior to Mr. Gaylord's settlement. The
time and place of Mr. Sturgeon's ordination remain to be dis-

* Webster, page 492.

covered. At a meeting of the Society, June 27th, the Monday following the supposed organization of the Church, Mr. Sturgeon appeared in the meeting of the Society and formally accepted the call. Wednesday, July 20th, was fixed upon for the installation. The Committee, appointed to make arrangements for the Council, consisted of Messrs. James Trowbridge, Joseph Birchard, Jonathan Elmer, Nathaniel Ketchum, John Taylor, Matthew St. John, and David Lambert. John Taylor and David Lambert were appointed " to provide for and entertain the Ministers and Messengers at the time of the Installment," and three months after were voted three pounds ten shillings for this service. The installation doubtless occurred on the day appointed.

It was a busy year. A house of worship must, if possible, be completed before winter. A house must be provided for the Pastor. Next Spring a military company must be organized, so that men need not go to Norwalk to drill. Highways, especially those leading to the Meeting-House, must be put in order ; perhaps some new ones opened, and this with as little cost as possible to the Society. One or two pounds for stray cattle must be provided. A tavern is needed, and in September, 1727, David Lambert is chosen " taverner."

The site chosen for the Meeting-House was on the south side of the upper road leading from Kent to Belden's Hill, near the present railroad track. This was then near the geographical center of the population. The dimensions of the building are not given. As no vote to erect it is recorded, the work was probably begun before the Society was organized. The burying-yard shall be near the Meeting-House, for we do not dream of a railroad and steam carriages plowing through it, as happened in 1851. The 30th of September the Society voted " that they would have their Meeting-House rectified by laying the floor, and by plastering the walls, and by making comfortable seats to set in." John Keeler and John St. John were appointed to get this work done. Deacon Hickok, Richard Bouton, John Dunning, John Stuart and Matthew St. John were appointed " to search out and agree for a convenient piece of land for an house lot" for the

Pastor. Matthew St. John was appointed a Committee on Meeting-House expenses.

It was thought that the General Assembly might, in consideration of these heavy burdens, abate the taxes of the Members of the Society for that year, and a committee was appointed in vain to look after the matter.

The work of finishing the Meeting-House made good progress. On the 30th of November, in accordance with the custom of those days, the Society voted " to seat it," and appointed a committee of three to "seat it by list and age, according to the best of their judgment." A delicate task which doubtless occasioned a good many heart-burnings. But in some form the plan was continued more than half a century longer. The order of seating nearly one hundred years ago has been preserved. Seven years later, in 1733, it was voted that John St. John should sit with Deacon Elmer "so long as he sets ye tune."

The matter of the Pastor's firewood must now be attended to; he has perhaps suffered in this winter weather. On the 20th of December the Society "voted that every man shall bring unto the Reverend Mr. Sturgeon a load of wood within fourteen days," and that any man who failed, should forfeit three shillings. How much wood this vote secured is not mentioned, but we fear that some men did not regard it, for the next December, A. D., 1727, it was voted that those who carried wood should have three shillings a load for good walnut, and two shillings and sixpence a load for good oak wood. The next December, 1728, it was voted to give Ebenezer Jackson nine pounds to furnish a sufficient supply of wood for Mr. Sturgeon, for the ensuing year. In February, 1730, it was voted that Mr. Sturgeon should have twenty-eight cords of wood annually. Here is something definite—better than glittering generalities, and yet some carper may say: "oak, hickory or chestnut?" and, "who is to bring it?"

The necessity of a school was soon felt. In December, 1728, the Ecclesiastical Society appointed Lieutenant Ketchum, Joseph Birchard and Ensign St. John "a Committee to set up a school or schools in the parish." It was voted to hire Mr. Sturgeon to teach; also to use the "country money," as far as it would go, and to require the scholars to make up the deficiency. Sixteen months later the parish was divided into three districts; Kent and Chestnut Hill formed one; Belden's Hill as far as James Stuart's, a second ; and "Pimpewalk" a third, each of which should receive one third of the country money. The School on Belden's Hill was to be taught in June and July, that in Pimpewalk, in August and September, and that in Kent "so long as their part [of the money] will come to." In order to increase the income of the Society, it was about this time "voted to have a flock among them, if they could get liberty from the town."

In Connecticut, till 1712, the towns had sole charge of school matters in their own bounds. Then the parish or Ecclesiastical Society (if that included only a portion of the town) had the care of their own territory. "In 1750, towns and societies were made practically equal in conducting school affairs." In 1798, and till 1856, the school society alone (and since 1856 the town alone, school societies having been then abolished) administered school matters, except such as were specially committed to the school district.

The law, from 1700 to 1820, required the towns to raise by tax the sum of forty shillings (except that from 1754 to 1767 it was less) on every thousand pounds of assessed property, for the use of schools in the town. The proceeds of this tax were known as "country money."

There were frequent votes respecting the schools. In January, 1792, the parish was divided into nine school districts. These were No. 1, Nod; No. 2, Bald Hill; No. 3, Middlebrook District; No. 4, Drum Hill; [Center District]; No. 6, Kent; No. 7, Pimpewaug; No. 8, Chestnut Hill; No. 9, Harry's Ridge. The Kent school-house stood in the triangle east of the Danbury road, and south of the "Old Burying-Ground" (as was customary), near the Meeting-House.*

After a time dissatisfaction with the "life and conversation " of Mr. Sturgeon so increased, that the Church consulted

---

* The tradition that it was once just north of the present Episcopal Church is, probably, not authentic.

the Association which met at Ripton (now Huntington), in November, 1731, and was advised to call a Council. This was agreed to in December. By Committee, an understanding with Mr. Sturgeon was reached ; but to complete the arrangement the Society's meeting adjourned to the last day of December, "at ye sun one hour high at night." Was that hour named to insure punctuality ?

There is no record of the dismission of Mr. Sturgeon ; but as the Society held a meeting in April, 1732, to adopt measures to obtain a minister, we may infer that the pastorate of Mr. Sturgeon ended the first of that month.

Not much has come to us of the personal appearance of Mr. Sturgeon, or of his sayings and doings. That he was able readily to find a text for a sermon is suggested in the tradition, that on the day of the arrival of his family, he preached from the words, "We have seen strange things to-day." There was evidently something in his manner of life and way of doing things that after a time made him unacceptable to the majority of his parishioners; but as they made no charges against him before the Council, we are permitted to believe that a lack of judgment, rather than any positive wrong-doing, led to his dismission. There is the more reason for this view, since he was afterwards connected with the Presbyterian Church, and settled for ten or twelve years, not very far from here, in Bedford, New York.* As a member of the Presbytery of New York, he was present at a meeting of the Synod in 1745. His name is not found in that connection after A.D. 1750. William Sturgeon, supposed to be a son of Rev. Robert Sturgeon, graduated at Yale, in the class of 1745, standing fourth in honor; and, having crossed the ocean, was ordained, in 1746, first deacon, and then priest, in the Church of England. He became assistant minister in Christ Church, Philadelphia, where he remained till 1766. He died in 1770.

The Society, April 11th, 1732, chose Deacons Trowbridge and Hickok and Jonathan Elmer a Committee " to advise

---

* Webster's History of the Presbyterian Church, page 492.

with ye Reverend ministers where to go for a minister, and empowered them to go or send for a minister at the cost of the Society."

They soon found Mr. William Gaylord, a graduate of Yale College in 1730, a licentiate of Hartford North Association, who was born November 29th, 1709, the son of Dea. William and Hopey Butler Gaylord, of "the West Division," in Hartford, now known as West Hartford. Mr. Gaylord was the great-grandson of that Dea. William Gaylord who came from England to Dorchester, Mass, in 1631. The Church of which he was Deacon was organized in Plymouth, England, January, 1630; and after remaining five years at Dorchester, it removed to Windsor, Conn., with its pastor, Rev. Mr. Warham, in September, 1636.* The mother of Mr. Gaylord was the granddaughter, or probably the great-granddaughter, of Rev. Samuel Stone, who was minister of the first church in Hartford thirty years, for fourteen of which he was the colleague of Rev. Thomas Hooker, the first Pastor. Mr. Hooker died in 1647, and Mr. Stone remained sole Pastor sixteen years longer. Mr. Gaylord was received to the Church, in West Hartford, in 1729. After as appears, three weeks of trial, Monday, May 29th, 1732, the Society invited Mr. Gaylord "to tarry with us some considerable time." Having called Mr. Sturgeon with too little consideration, they would be more circumspect in choosing a second Pastor. On Friday of the same week, the Society voted to give Mr. Gaylord four pounds ten shillings for "preaching among us three Sabbaths." Three months later, August 29th, the Society voted to call Mr. Gaylord to settle in the work of the Gospel ministry. It was also agreed to buy the house and land of Mr. Sturgeon. Joseph Birchard, Captain Ketchum and Matthew St. John were appointed to carry out the vote. The Church was unanimous in calling Mr. Gaylord.

But there was apparently some difficulty in Mr. Gaylord's mind as to accepting the call. Possibly, the neglect to name

* Dr. Hawes in Conn. Eccl. Col., page 86.

any salary embarrassed him. Six weeks later a new Committee were appointed "to treat with Mr. Gaylord as to terms of settlement and salary." November 1st the call to settle is renewed by "a universal vote." Two weeks later the Society voted that the salary should be "four pence half penny upon the pound until four pence half penny makes one hundred and thirty pounds, to be paid, either in money or in provisions at the market price, and that to be a standing salary so long as he carries on the work of the ministry among us." Mr. Gaylord accepted the call, but did not accept the salary, and that was afterwards voted annually.

In accordance with a custom of those days, which was not altogether abandoned till about fifty years ago, the Society also voted, as a gift, or "settlement," as it was called, two hundred pounds. This was to enable a young minister to purchase a house, land, furniture, books, and whatever else might be needed to set up housekeeping, and carry on his parish work, which it was hoped and expected would terminate only with his life.

In Mr. Gaylord's case the Society afterwards voted to present him the house and land purchased of Mr. Sturgeon, in lieu of one hundred and sixty of the two hundred pounds promised. But since Mr. Sturgeon had left so soon, and his religious opinions, perhaps, were not all in harmony with the Westminster Catechism, or at least with the Saybrook Platform; and inasmuch as the Society could ill afford to give a new minister a settlement every few years, it was considerately provided, "That if Mr. Gaylord turn from ye opinion or principles he now professes, contrary to ye mind of ye Society, then he is to return to ye Society ye two hundred pounds again." In December a salary "at the rate of sixty-five pounds for ye year was voted." Two years later, 1734, the salary was made for that year one hundred pounds, to be paid in money or provisions at the market price.

The arrangements for the Pastor's support having been satisfactorily made, preparations for the Ordination were in order. The Council met on the afternoon of the 13th of February, 1733. The day was short. Some of the members had ridden, probably, on horseback twenty miles. An evening session would not be convenient. An organization was effected by choosing for Moderator, Rev. Thomas Hawley, of Ridgefield, who was then in the twenty-first year of his pastorate; and for Scribe, Rev. Samuel Cooke, who had been Pastor at Stratfield above seventeen years. On Wednesday morning, February 14th, the Council reassembled. We are interested to know their names. From Stratfield (now Bridgeport), with Mr. Cooke came Capt. David Sherman; from Ridgefield, with Mr. Hawley. Dea. Thomas Smith; from Norwalk, Rev. Moses Dickinson; from Stratford, Rev. Hezekiah Gold and Mr. Ephraim Clark; from Stamford, Rev. Ebenezer Wright and Lieut. Samuel Weed; from Greenfield, Rev. John Goodsell and Mr. John Burr; and later in the day, from Greensfarms, Capt. Thomas Nash. The lay delegates in the minutes are styled Messengers.

A careful examination of Mr. Gaylord followed, "as to his end in undertaking the ministry," and his doctrinal belief, his views of Church polity and his acceptance of the Confession of Faith. In these matters they received "good satisfaction." To the Saybrook Platform Mr. Gaylord in substance assented. The order of Ordination exercises was as follows: Mr. Goodsell made the opening prayer; Mr. Hawley preached; Mr. Cooke offered the ordaining prayer; Mr. Dickinson gave the charge; Mr. Wright gave the Right Hand. We miss the "Address to the People," which was not then customary.

Three weeks before the ordination, Mr. Gaylord was united in marriage with Elizabeth Davenport. She was the youngest daughter of the Rev. John Davenport, the fourth Pastor of the Church in Stamford, where he ministered nearly thirty-seven years, till his death in 1731. He was the only son of the only son of that famous Rev. John Davenport, who was the first Pastor of the first Church in New Haven, from 1639 to 1667, and was one of the Synod which, by the order of the General Court of Connecticut, met in 1708 at Saybrook and constructed the Saybrook Platform, by which the ecclesiastical affairs of the Congregational Churches, of this and some other Counties, are still regulated. Mr. Davenport was one of the most prominent and influential men in Connecticut in that generation. His death was spoken of as "the removal of one eminent for learning, and who was a bulwark and barrier upon our frontiers."

Fourteen years after her marriage Mrs. Gaylord died, probably from pulmonary consumption, leaving six children, and having buried one. Her husband's eulogy on the Church records is honorable to both. It begins thus: "A good God has made her a good wife to me, both in spirituals and temporals, prudent, faithful, loving, loyal, and very respectful." Her oldest son, William Gaylord, is said to have lived for a time in West Hartford, but is mentioned in his father's will as a resident of New Hartford.

We are indebted to Mr. Gaylord for about thirty-three years of well kept Church records, containing the names of the members of the Church, and the families of the congregation with their children, at the time of his ordination; the members of the Church in full and by the Half-Way Covenant; a list of marriages, baptisms and deaths, with occasional remarks.

From this record it appears that there were on the 14th of February, 1733, thirty-five men and forty-one women in full communion. How many of these were original members, how many had been added, how many dismissed and died during the six and a half preceding years, we have no means of knowing. It is worth noting that the thirty-five men, each had a wife, though in two cases the wife entered the Church after this date. The women, too, had each a husband. Of those who had owned the covenant, as their half way confession of faith was called, there were ten men and seven women. Of these ten, four of the men were without wives, or else their wives had refused to own the covenant. Each of the seven women had a husband; but one of the husbands was already in full communion, and his wife afterwards united. There are on the list thirty-two families, but not a widow or widower among them. There is some reason to believe that the list does not contain all the families in the parish. The name of Dea. James Trowbridge and of Dea.

Matthew Gregory does not occur. Of the fifty-one or fifty-two husbands and wives enrolled, only six or seven couple were neither of them connected with the Church. Of children whose names are given with their parents, there are one hundred and thirty-seven, of whom eighty-seven were boys and fifty girls—a disproportion not too great to meet the sad waste of war in the fifty years that followed. The whole number of names exceeds two hundred.

As families increased, new roads and bridges became necessary. In 1735 it was voted to open a highway—where probably there had been only a cart-path—to Buckingham's Ridge—which has sometimes been called Harty's Ridge—east of Hurlbutt street. Four years later (December 14th, 1739) the town is asked to build a horse-bridge across the Norwalk river, in Pimpewaug, near Capt. St. John's house, to repair the horse-bridge near John Marvin's dwelling-house in Kent, and to complete the bridge already begun by the Wilton people near the house of Eliakim Elmer on the Ridgefield road. The town votes to build the Pimpewaug and to repair the Kent bridge, but no action as to the other bridge implies, that we are permitted to complete it without town aid. Capt. Matthew St. John and Joseph Platt are appointed a Committee to build the one and repair the other bridge. Five years later David Deforest was appointed in Mr. (now Captain) Platt's place. The next year David Keeler is chosen in the room of Captain St. John, and the year following (1746) Benjamin Betts is chosen, in the room of David Keeler, "to take care of ye bridge at Wilton, near Lieut. John Marvin's dwelling-house." Bridge building that will endure the rage of the Norwalk river in Spring freshets was no child's play in those days.

Soon after Mr. Gaylord's settlement a new difficulty arose. The parish grows. The minister is popular. The Meeting-House is too small, and not conveniently located. December 25, 1736, it was voted to build a new Meeting-House forty-six feet long, thirty-five feet wide, with twenty feet posts, to be placed on what in the record is called "Sharp Hill," but which for above half a century has now been known as "the old burying-ground." A large oak yet marks the spot, sole survivor of the trees and shrubbery once there, and a silent sentinel over the graves of three generations. May no woodman's axe ever be lifted against it. The want of funds probably caused the delay to build at once. November 18th, 1737, it was voted to build a house forty-eight by thirty-five feet and twenty-two feet posts ; and also to raise by taxes one hundred pounds for building purposes. Of the land needed for the site, John Marvin, Sr., gave eight rods square ; and seventeen years later (1755) Richard Dunning* sold above half an acre, for a burial place, for fifty pounds, old tenor. No plan of this house is known to exist, but the vote was that the front or broadside should face the south. In June, 1739, David Keeler was appointed auctioneer to sell the old house. David Keeler, Daniel Betts and Matthew Marvin were to receive one hundred and fifty pounds "to be improved towards walling and glazing the Meeting House and other things necessary." In December it was voted that the money for which the old Meeting-House sold should be paid to the same Committee, to aid in finishing, the new house. But it is easier for us to vote money than to raise it ; for two years later (December, 1741) it is soon enough to vote "that in finishing their Meeting-House" they "will observe ye former model that the Prime Ancient Society of Norwalk hath done in finishing theirs," and " that the pews around the body of ye house be six feet square." It was not till 1743, that the seats were in readiness to receive persons, in the order designated by the Committee, and not till 1747 that the vote was passed, by which the galleries should be finished and be made of "good, white wood and white oak boards," "with one seat round the front," and "one tier of pews round the house."

Meantime a wonderful revival of religion was going forward in New England and elsewhere, in which Wilton shared. This awakening began in Northampton, Mass., as early as 1679, and recurred on several occasions afterwards,

---

* Richard Dunning is supposed to have lived in the house south of the burying-ground, now occupied by Charles Comstock.

and especially in 1735, and again in 1740, under the ministry
of Jonathan Edwards. Two years after the ordination of
Mr. Gaylord special religious interest was manifest in Lebanon, in a part of the town which is now Columbia; the
Pastor of which, Rev. Eleazer Wheelock, who was in full
sympathy with Mr. Edwards, distinguished himself greatly
by the abundance of his labors and the power of his preaching in Eastern Connecticut.   Now, it happened that Mr.
Wheelock—who was some two years younger than Mr. Gaylord, and who became afterwards the founder and first
President of Dartmouth College—married, in 1735, the widow
Sarah Maltby, of New Haven, who was a daughter of Rev.
John Davenport and a sister of Mrs. Gaylord.*   It would be
most natural that Dr. Wheelock's zeal and spiritual activity
should be felt through his Brother Gaylord in Wilton.   Mr.
Whitfield, then on his second visit to this country, while
going from New Haven to New York in the Autumn of
1740, preached in the new unfinished Meeting-House in this
place.   The next two years a considerable number was added
to the Church.

But the revivals excited much bitterness and violent opposition in many towns.   Their promoters were, in derision,
called the "New Lights."   In some cases their conduct was
not tempered with sound judgment.   But the "Old Lights"
were sometimes neither conciliatory or wise, so that in Eastern Connecticut several new Churches, known as "Separate
Churches," were formed.   The feeling of opposition to the
revival, and especially to the evils which seemed to attend it,
was so wide-spread and bitter, that in May, 1742, a law was
passed forbidding, under heavy penalty, the minister of one
parish to preach in another parish, except upon invitation of
the minister thereof.   The people of North Coventry had no
Pastor, and had not yet organized a Church.   Therefore, the
Society voted that any one of twenty-four ministers named
might, upon invitation, preach or exhort at any time in that

---

* Another sister, Abigail Davenport, married Rev. Stephen Williams, D.D., Pastor
of the Church in Longmeadow, Mass., who was a son of that Rev. John Williams,
of Deerfield, that was carried captive by the Indians, and was sixty-six years a
minister.

parish; and also "voted that any Church member, or any head of family, may invite any of the above ministers to preach in said Society."

But Rev. Dr. Pomroy, of Hebron—a near neighbor of Mr. Wheelock, an eloquent preacher and a man of much worth and weight of character—was prosecuted and fined, by the loss of his salary seven years, because he preached in a grove in Colchester, without the consent of the Pastor, Mr. Little, who did not belong to the "New Lights," but with whom he had always been on friendly terms. Indeed he supposed, until he reached Colchester on that occasion, that Mr. Little consented to his coming. The Wilton Church and its Pastor happily escaped these disturbances, and the Churches of this County were for the most part exempt from the strife, which the "Old Lights," who were afraid of revivals and especially of the fanaticism they occasionally excited, sometimes stirred up. The contention was really between a dead orthodoxy and the Spirit of the Lord; and the Pastor of this Church and his people were blessed by yielding to the Spirit.

But religious controversy was not the only occasion of trouble and sorrow to our fathers of that period. There was war, and there were rumors of war. In 1739, while this Society was building the second Meeting-House, the Colonies were involved in a war between Great Britain and her old enemies, France and Spain. A military expedition was sent to the West Indies. Six years later Connecticut and Massachusetts contributed largely of men and money, to an enterprise which resulted in the capture, from the French, of Cape Breton and the strong fortress of Louisburg. This provoked France to equip, the next year, 1746, a powerful fleet, on which embarked many thousand troops, with the avowed design of burning and laying waste New England. Against such an armament the Colonies possessed no means of successful defence, and were in great alarm, especially in Eastern Massachusetts. They turned, therefore, to Almighty God for help. The answers to their prayers were most gracious. Storms, the sickness of the French troops, the suicide of the First Admiral and afterwards of the Second, delayed, scattered, and rendered impotent the fleet, so that it returned in ignominy to France, without having fired a gun against this people. The next year France sent another expedition, which was met and vanquished by an English fleet. But it was not till 1748, when Great Britain and France made peace at Aix-la-Chapelle, that the nine years of anxiety and loss ended. Even then heavy taxes remained, and a depreciated currency. Until 1740 the bills or currency of the Colony, known as "old tenor," were based upon taxes levied, and worth their face in specie. After 1740 the increase of bills to meet war expenses, without laying taxes sufficient to pay them, occasioned a serious depreciation. Eighty thousand pounds of Government "promises to pay," known as "new tenor," supplemented by no provision for paying, could no more then than now, supply the place of gold and silver. Mr. Gaylord's salary furnishes an illustration: The first year it was sixty-five pounds; the second one hundred. In 1747 and 1748 it was by vote four hundred pounds. In 1749 it was five hundred pounds; the next two years six hundred and fifty pounds annually—that is, the currency had fallen to one-sixth or less of its nominal value. In 1751 Parliament prohibited the Colonies from further issue of paper currency, and gradually the bills were redeemed. In 1755 Mr. Gaylord's salary was only fifty-five pounds, and the next year sixty pounds, for silver was again the standard. The remainder of his ministry it ranged from fifty to seventy-five pounds. It needs no old journal, or letters from Pastor or people, to persuade us that this fluctuation of the currency caused much trouble and suffering. The catalogue shows that the spiritual interests of the Church suffered. The number of admissions to its communion was small during those years.

Hardly had the financial skies cleared, when another and heavier storm of war burst upon the country, and raged for eight years, sweeping away thousands of precious lives and much treasure. This is known as the French and Indian war, which was occasioned by the plan of the French Government, to stretch a line of forts and trading posts, from Canada to the mouth of the Mississippi. By this means, France de-signed to erect a barrier to the growth of the Colonies westward and southwestward, and secure for itself the Valley of the Miss-issippi and also the profitable trade with the Indians.

But already the English looked with covetous eyes upon the territory west of the Alleghanies. The sword must de-cide who should possess it.

In this war, Connecticut furnished a large number of men. Namely, one thousand in 1755, and twenty-five hundred the next year. The succeeding year fourteen hundred men were called for, and five thousand were raised; and in 1758 five thousand, besides a thousand others sent to Western Massa-chusetts, as militia to guard the frontier. But now, seeing that Parliament did not, as was expected, furnish money to pay the troops, the taxes began to increase. The people of Connecticut had had enough of irredeemable paper money; so, with each issue of bills, went out the law for tax-ation to meet them. In 1758 the tax was nine pence on the pound, and then five pence per pound additional, making a tax nearly equal to six cents on the dollar. The next year four thousand men were voted, and also a tax of ten pence on the pound to be paid four years later. The trial was the greater because for the first three years it seemed like wasting money and lives. The incompetence of the English adminis-tration, and of many of the English officers, who were selected on much the same principle that for some years men have been in this country appointed to office, occasioned disaster and humiliating defeats. But when, in 1758, William Pitt became Prime Minister and reformed the English military service, the tide changed. The enemy were driven from West-ern Pennsylvania and Northern New York; from Quebec by Wolf in 1759, and from Canada in 1760; on which account we had in Connecticut a special Thanksgiving, October 23d, 1760.

But war-like operations and the call for troops continued two years longer, till terms of peace were signed in February, 1763. Then for a time, except from Indian depredations in Northern New York and Western Pennsylvania, there is

quiet in all our borders. The men who were active in that
war were known to our grandfathers and great-grandfathers, but
few of their names have been preserved on the Wilton records.
The men who enlisted were, of course, credited to Norwalk.
But aside from others, one death came sharply to Mr. Gaylord.
Under date, October, 7, 1760, in the obituary list he writes:
" *Moses Gaylord,* aged twenty-one years," and adds: " He died
at Fort Herkimer on his way from Oswego to Albany, after
he had been from home in ye expedition against Montreal, a·
little more than four months, and after above two months of
sore sickness at Oswego on his way toward Albany." There
are four * others who died the same year, who were probably soldiers, two of them at Schenectady, one of whom was
Captain Thaddeus Mead.

While his dear son Moses was dying at Fort Herkimer,
the family of Mr. Gaylord were blessed by the birth of another
son, who received the significant name "Deodate," "Gift
of God," who passed his whole life in Wilton, and died in
1840 at the age of eighty. Between the birth of the father
and death of the son, one hundred and thirty years intervened.
Mr. Deodate Gaylord is well remembered by many who are
here. His daughter, Mrs. Charles Davenport, honored and beloved, still has her home in Wilton, and in her son we joy-
fully welcome the poet laureate of this Anniversary.

In December, 1766, Mr. Gaylord's health was so much impaired, that the Society voted to employ an assistant. But,
as it would seem, before one could be obtained, disease made
rapid progress, and he died January 2, 1767, aged fifty-seven
years; having been Pastor of the Church nearly thirty-four
years. He was buried near the Church, where his memorial
stone, bearing an honorable inscription, still stands. His Pastorate was longer than any other in this Church, and, with two
exceptions, double the length of any. He was the only Pastor, beside Mr. Ball, who has died in office, and the only Pastor
whose dust hallows the burying-ground of this Society.

Mr. Gaylord was evidently a man of public spirit, and

---

* Abraham Higgins, 20 years ; Abijah Hubbell, 25 years ; Josiah Canfield.

held in high esteem by his brethren in the Ministry. He was methodical and exact in his mode of life, as the Church records, now invaluable as an exponent of his Ministry, attest. Of the General Association, which yesterday closed its one hundred and sixty-seventh Anniversary, at Norwalk, he was six times a member, the first time at Hartford in 1740, the last at Lyme in 1763. In 1751, at Windham, he was Moderator. He was sound in faith, not a man of extreme views, and probably would be reckoned a moderate Calvinist. His epitaph gives him the honorable appellation of peacemaker. He was not remarkably demonstrative in his mode of speaking. A tradition, I know not how authentic, states, that when, on one occasion, he preached in Ridgefield, on exchange with the Rev. Jonathan Ingersoll, the great grandfather of the present honored Governor of Connecticut, who was thirty-eight years pastor there, the people in Ridgefield spoke of the sermon as uninteresting. When opportunity offered, Mr. Ingersoll borrowed the sermon of Mr. Gaylord, and, without comment, preached it to his people. When the people praised it as superior to Mr. Gaylord's from the same text, Mr. Ingersoll replied, "he could always preach well, when he could get one of Mr. Gaylord's sermons to preach."

The parish grew and prospered under Mr. Gaylord's ministry, and was fairly united. The record shows above nine hundred baptisms (924 or more). Most of those baptized were young children, as the Half-Way Covenant prevailed, and most who statedly attended public worship brought their children for baptism. They were usually presented on the Sabbath, and sometimes on more than one Sunday of the same month. The record of deaths testifies to the general good health of the people. The average number recorded during the first twelve years of Mr. Gaylord's ministry was 4.5 per year, the next ten years 6.8. Among the deaths were the two eldest daughters of Mr. Gaylord. Their disease was consumption.

There were on the list 183 weddings. The marriage fee ranged, as I read the record, from eighteen pence to forty shillings. Mr. Gaylord's second wife was Elizabeth Bishop.

There were born to him thirteen children. Mrs. Gaylord survived her husband forty-five years.

After the death of Mr. Gaylord, the Society again applied to the Association. Mr. Samuel Mills preached as a candidate. On the fifth of March, 1767, the Society voted to call Mr. Mills, fifteen in the negative. The first of July they again voted ; " a great majority, only fourteen in the negative," says the record. In October they repeated the call, " only fourteen in the negative." The Clerk of the Society evidently was not with the fourteen. Still Mr. Mills did not accept, and in February the Society made one effort more. They appointed a large Committee to wait upon Mr. Mills, and if he could not be obtained, to seek another candidate. Mr. Mills was evidently determined not to become the Pastor of a divided people, and so he finally declined.

There lives in Wilton no tradition of this Mr. Mills, whence he came or whither he went, yet his excellence was so apparent, that the people would persist in calling him about once a quarter for a whole year.

There seems no reason to doubt that this young man was the now famous Rev. Samuel J. Mills, better known as "Father Mills of Torringford." He was born May 16th, 1743, graduated at Yale College in 1764, was licensed by the Association of Litchfield County in 1766, and in September, 1768, was examined and commended to the Church in Torringford, where he was settled in 1769, and remained the Minister of that Church sixty-four years, till his death forty-three years ago, at the age of ninety years. Six years ago that Church made a grand centennial celebration of the settlement of Father Mills,* who, though no longer in the flesh, walks in the spirit, not the streets of Torringford only, but the hills and valleys of Litchfield County, living in the traditions of ministers and people, and often heard at their meetings of Association and Conference. His mother, Jane Lewis Mills, was a native of Stratford. In his biography no mention is made of his preaching in Wilton. That year is unaccounted for.

---

* The Historical Address was delivered by Rev. William H. Moore, and, with other proceedings of the occasion, published.

Mr. Mills was tall and large, dignified in manner, and rode on horseback like a general—the admiration of all horsemen.* His eyes were large and beaming, his voice rich and powerful. At times he was mighty in eloquence. He was frequently irresistably comic in his language and unexpected turns of thought; at other times he suddenly brought tears to eyes unused to weep, or awed his hearers by sudden disclosures of the Majesty of the Most High, and of the awful solemnities of eternity. He has a special interest to us; because his son, who bore his name, was associated with Gordon Hall and James Richards and others in praying and planning, at Williams College and at Andover, till the American Board began to be and to send the Gospel to the heathen; and still further because the present Pastor of this Church, named from the son, perpetuates and honors the name of Samuel J. Mills.

In May, 1768, the Society invited Mr. ISAAC LEWIS to preach as a candidate. Mr. Lewis† was born in that part of Stratford, now Huntington, January 21 (O. S.), 1746. He graduated at Yale in 1765, in a class of which twenty-one out of forty-seven became Ministers of the Gospel. He studied Divinity at East Hampton, L. I., and was licensed to preach by Fairfield East Association, in Danbury, March, 1768. He soon received a call to Newport, R. I., to the Church over which the renowned Dr. Hopkins was subsequently settled. But the unanimous call of this Society, and probably of the Church, ‡ given in May, to preach upon probation, was accepted. The nearness of Wilton to his father's residence may have influenced his decision to remain in Connecticut. In July, the Society voted to call Mr. Isaac Lewis into the work of the Ministry. There was some difficulty in fixing the salary. Eleven voted against the call, not from dislike to Mr. Lewis, but because they preferred the old method of voting the salary year by year. "A stated salary" was not to their mind. One hundred and fifty pounds were voted as a settlement, and seventy pounds as the first year's salary. Lieutenant Nehemiah Mead, Nathan

---

Stuart and Ezra Gregory were appointed a Committee to make arrangements for the ordination, which occurred Tuesday, October, 26th, 1768. Rev. Jedediah Mills preached the sermon.*   He had been Mr. Lewis' pastor and instructor in fitting for College; was settled at Huntington two years before the organization of this Church, and continued there till his death in 1776.

December, 1768, Mr. Lewis married Miss Hannah Beale, daughter of Matthew Beale, of New Preston—a lady well fitted for her new position. He occupied a house in Kent; afterwards, and till his death, May 10th, 1845, occupied by Capt. Daniel Betts, which was pulled down a few years ago. It was the second house south of the junction of the Ridgefield and Danbury road, on the west side of the street.

The records show that, notwithstanding the unsettled state of public affairs, Mr. Lewis' ministry was neither barren nor unfruitful.   In 1773 his salary was increased to ninety pounds. A majority also voted to build a new house of worship. When Mr. Lewis was settled, the country already felt the ground-swell of the Revolution, and he shared with his people the anxiety and losses that came with the war. In 1776 he was appointed Chaplain of a Connecticut regiment, commanded by Col. Philip B. Bradley, which was stationed at Bergen, N. J. After seven months service, he was so severely attacked by a fever that his life was despaired of. Afterwards he received the appointment of Chaplain in the Continental army ; but, as the Wilton people were unwilling to give him leave of absence, he did not accept it. When the British were about to land at Norwalk in 1779, he went at the head of a company of men to resist, and a cannon

---

* On the Council were : Rev. Moses Dickinson, 1727-1778, Mr. Samuel Fitch, Norwalk ; Rev. Noah Hobart 1733-73, Samuel Rowland, Fairfield ; Rev. Abraham Todd, Greenwich, 1734-1773, Second Church ; Rev. Jonathan Ingersoll 1740-1778; Deacon John Benedict, Ridgefield ; Rev. Robert Silliman, 1742-'71 (1) ; Theophilus Fitch, [New] Canaan.   Rev.   Moses   Mather,   1744-1805 ;   Jonathan   Selleck,   Darien ;   Rev. Samuel Sherwood, 1757-1783, Weston; Rev. Seth Pomeroy, in 1758-1769, Greenfield ; Rev. William Tennent, colleague of Mr. Dickinson, 1765-1772 ; Rev. Hezekiah Ripley, 1767-1821, Dea. Thomas Nash, Greensfarms ; Rev. Ebenezer Davenport, 1767-1773, Greenwich, First Church.

(1) Dr. David Willard, the grandson of Mr. Silliman, was, from 1812 to his death in 1860, a resident of Wilton, and a practicing physician forty-five years; also a member of the Church from 1822.

ball struck within three feet of him. After Norwalk was burned the people appointed a day of fasting and prayer, and as the old Pastor (Mr. Dickinson) had died the year before, Mr. Lewis preached to them in an unfinished house which had escaped the flames.

At one time, that he might preach in destitute places, he exchanged with the minister in Dorset, Vermont, for several weeks, and visited places in that region during the week. Connecticut ministers, by appointment of General Association, did much missionary circuit preaching in Vermont before the formation of the Connecticut Missionary Society in 1798. Before his missionary work was quite complete, Mr. Lewis had nearly lost his life by the breaking of a blood-vessel. Happily, he reached home alive and recovered completely from the disease. He had a highly advantageous offer to go to South Carolina, but declined, as he said, because of his "strong disapprobation of the system of slavery."

Mr. Lewis, as well as the people, felt severely the derangement in the currency produced by the war. In 1777 his salary was made one hundred pounds, lawful money, one-half to be paid in provisions, the prices of which were fixed and low. For example: Wheat was to be seventy-five cents a bushel; beef, two dollars and a half a hundred; leather shoes, one dollar a pair. But the next year, while the salary was the same, wheat was one dollar and sixty-seven cents per bushel; rye had increased twenty per cent.; pork, twenty per cent.; beef was to be two cents per pound in the autumn and three cents per pound in the winter. Four years later (1782) it was voted that the salary be one hundred pounds, lawful money, to be paid in silver or gold. During these later years the financial difficulties of the country were so great, that it became necessary for the towns to assume the support, at least in part, of their own soldiers in the Continental army. Accounts kept by Abijah Betts—the maternal grandfather of our honored townsman, Capt. Abijah Betts, now living in Kent—are in the possession of his family. These give the names of officers and soldiers who received provisions and articles of clothing by this agency.*

Aside from other afflictions of the war, Wilton suffered from actual invasion when the British passed through on the occasion of the burning of Danbury in April, 1777. On their return, hungry and weary with marching and fighting, they entered many houses for food. As they came down the Ridgefield road, they fired a ball into the house of Dea. Daniel Gregory, in which were his wife and children. The eldest, Abigail—afterwards the wife of Moses Gregory—when above eighty years of age, was accustomed to tell how an officer came in, with his sword drawn, attended by soldiers. He assured them of safety if they would furnish food. The British set fire to the house near the Episcopal Church, now occupied by Mr. Sherman Fitch; but, before they were out of sight, a woman went with a pail of water from the next house north (which has lately fallen down, but was for many years occupied by Major Samuel Belden), and extinguished the flames. As people heard of the approach of the British they hastily removed their silver spoons and such valuable property as they could. From houses on the Belden's Hill road, furniture was carried to Huckleberry Hills, as it was supposed the British might take that street; but learning, as it would seem, that soldiers were gathering at Norwalk, the

---

* From these memoranda it appears that the following persons were in the army a part or the whole of the periods 1780-1783: Capt. Samuel Comstock (afterwards Major), Lieut. Samuel Deforest, Ensign (in 1782 Lieut.) Matthew Gregory, Seth Hubbell, Samuel Nichols, Jesse Olmstead, Ambrose Barns, John Johnson, John Williams, Jonathan Jackson, Elijah Betts; and in 1782 Lieut. Salmon Hubbell and Uriah Mead. Elijah Taylor is elsewhere mentioned as Ensign.(1) A warning is also found written and signed by Samuel Comstock, Captain Ninth (?) Regiment, calling his company together for inspection the 17th of October, 1776. Washington was at that time at White Plains, after the retreat from Long Island. He had called most of the Connecticut troops to his aid As Lieut. Gregory was in the action at White Plains the 28th of October, it is probable that Capt. Comstock marched thither with his company directly after the 17th. Major Comstock represented Norwalk in the L egis-lature, October, 1800, and Wilton in eight Sessions, between October, 1803, and May, 1809. In his will he gave to the Church, for its Communion service, a silver tankard which had for generations been an heirloom in the family. He was born 1739, the son of Dea. Nathan Comstock, and, as is supposed, in the house so long occupied by Edward Comstock. He died December 1st, 1824, in his 86th year. He enlisted July 10th, 1775, and was commissioned Captain, July 10th, 1776. He and his company shared in the sufferings of Valley Forge, in the battle of Monmouth, and the capture of Cornwallis. His wife was Mercy Mead, daughter of Theophilus Mead. Lieut. Matthew Gregory, the son of Ezra and grandson of Dea. Matthew Gregory, was with Major Comstock in the places just mentioned, and was also in the fight at Ridgefield, April 27th, 1777. His death occurred in his ninety-first year, June 4th, 1848, at Albany, N. Y., where he had resided forty years or more. His first wife, Mary, daughter of Hezekiah Deforest, died in 1796.

(1) In records in Comptroller's Office, Hartford, says Hon. William Edgar Raymond, to whom I am indebted for facts respecting Major Comstock.

enemy took the Westport road, and, finding Westport already occupied by several hundred Americans, they turned east, crossed the Saugatuck river about three miles above the bridge, marched to Compo, and got on shipboard that night. It was their last attempt to go far from the shore in Con-necticut. But the Wilton people suffered afterwards in the burning of Norwalk, though their houses and their lives were spared.

After the war ended, a new difficulty arose. The "Half-Way Covenant," as it was called, had in the preceding century been adopted by many Churches in Connecticut and Massachusetts. The principle of this covenant, briefly stated, was that those who had been baptized in infancy, when grown to riper years, if "they understand the ground of religion, and are not scandalous, and solemnly own their covenant with the Church (into which covenant baptism introduced them)," "might dedicate their children to the Lord in baptism." And this, though they did not believe themselves converted persons, and did not propose to come to the Lord's table! This theory was not at first generally acceptable to the New England Churches. In order to give it currency it was found necessary to convene a Synod at Boston in 1662, which, by a majority vote, recommended it. Many Churches accepted it with great reluctance, and some refused altogether. President Edwards showed that it was unscriptural. The revivals of that generation, by making the distinction between converted and unconverted men more manifest, prepared the churches to reject it on two grounds: first, that that covenant was contrary to the Gospel; and second, that trouble had arisen by the influence of uncon-verted men thus openly recognized as Church members. Mr. Lewis persuaded this Church to consider the question of giving up the Half-Way Covenant.

A meeting was held October 30th, 1783, and continued by successive adjournments to the 4th of December of the same year, when, after much discussion, it was voted (1.) unanimously that, in the opinion of this Church, no person ought to be admitted to the enjoyment of the special

ordinances of the Gospel; but such as appear to be real
Christians. (2.) The Church consents to abolish or discontinue
what is commonly called the half way practice. (3.) The
Church will not treat those in the Half-Way Covenant as
outcasts, but is ready to receive them to Communion when
they request, providing their conduct is good. The second
and third votes were not unanimous. It is easy to see that
worldly men—who enjoyed most of the privileges, without the
responsibilities, of Church membership—would not regard
with pleasure this movement, which left them without even a
name to live; but they were members of the Society, and,
though Mr. Lewis seems to have been popular before, they
"testified their dissatisfaction by withholding from him,
either altogether or in a great measure, the salary they had
pledged him."* Possibly, had the discussion of the subject
not occurred till after the annual meeting of the Society the
result might have been somewhat different. After three
years the Consociation was called to hear the case, and Mr.
Lewis, at his own request, was dismissed June 1st, 1786. His
ministry lasted about eighteen years, during which three
hundred and eighty-two persons were baptized; fifty-nine renewed the covenant, and sixty-four were received to Communion. When the condition of the country and the
experience of many other Churches during that period are
considered, it will be seen that his ministry was more than
usually successful.† It is evident that the Consociation so
judged, for on the day of his dismission he was invited to
preach in Greenwich. Some of the Wilton people were
desirous that he should still be their Pastor, but in the
October following he was installed as Pastor of the Second
Church in Greenwich, where he remained thirty-two years,
till, in the seventy-third year of his age and the fifty-first of
his ministry, by his own urgent request, the Consociation was
called. He was dismissed December 1st, 1818, and the same
day his son, the Rev. Isaac Lewis, Junior, who had been

---

* Many families, no doubt, voluntarily continued to pay their proportion of the salary, and he was accustomed to fit young men for College. Dea. Matthew Marvin
fitted with him.

† Sprague's Annals.

preaching at New Rochelle, was installed his successor, where he continued ten years. Mr. Lewis (the father) received the degree of Doctor of Divinity from Yale College in 1792. After his dismission he remained in Greenwich till his death, August 27th, 1840. He was for a year or two a member of the Corporation of the College. He died in the ninety-fourth year of his age and the seventy-third year of his ministry. In 1830, when Rev. Joel Mann was settled at Greenwich, Dr. Lewis gave the charge to the people, which was his last public service, except occasional addresses at the Communion table. The sermon at his funeral was preached by the Pastor of the Church, Rev. Noah Coe, from 1 Cor. 3 : 11; the same text from "which Mr. Whitfield preached the sermon in Yale College Chapel, which had been the means of awakening his mind to religion more than three-quarters of a century before."

To Dr. Lewis were born nine children, six of whom were sons. Two of the sons (Zechariah and Isaac) were twins, born in Wilton, January 1st, 1773. They, as also a brother, graduated at Yale College.* Mrs. Lewis died April 13th, 1829.

Rev. Nathaniel Hewitt, once so well known here as the first Pastor of the Second Church in Bridgeport, thus describes Dr. Lewis' appearance in 1818, the year of his dismission from Greenwich : "In January, 1818, I was installed at Fairfield, where I met, for the first time, the late Rev. Dr. Isaac Lewis. He took part in the public solemnities on that occasion, and offered the installing prayer.* * * In his person and deportment he united the Patriarch, Prophet and Saint. His head and shoulders were above his brethren, and his hair flowing and white as the snow; his shoulders, broad; his forehead, massive; his complexion, so clear and pure as to resemble a child's; a large, blue eye, expressive of mildness and purity; his voice, smooth and guttural; and his

---

* Zechariah Lewis studied theology, but was unable to preach on account of his health. He was Tutor in Yale (1796–1799), Editor, Secretary of the New York Religious Tract Society, &c., and died in Brooklyn, N. Y., November 14th, 1840, aged sixty-seven years. Isaac Lewis, Jr., studied theology in New Haven, was ordained May 30, 1798, preached in Cooperstown and Goshen, N. Y., at Bristol, R. I., at New Rochelle, and in Greenwich, 1818 to 1828. He received D. D. from Delaware College in 1844. He died in New York, September 23d, 1854, aged eighty-one years. One of the sons died in infancy ; the other three were lawyers.—Sprague, Vol. 1, pp. 666–67.

air and attitude, in the pulpit and in prayer, more as a
man of God than any other I have ever known."

A little more than two months after the dismission of Mr.
Lewis from this Church, after a warm discussion, the Church
voted, August 9th, 1786, to revoke their vote to abolish the
Half-Way Covenant, and September 28th, 1786, to restore
the Half-Way Covenant, according to the vote of 1770; but
a few years after the Churches had, by common consent, given
up that plan, and this Church, under the lead of Mr. Fisher,
among them. The result of the course of the majority of the
Society, in securing the dismission of Mr. Lewis, illustrates
that societies and individuals often have it in their power to
do things it were unwise to do. Several years elapsed before
the Church could agree upon a minister, who would accept
their call.* The salary was small, money was hard to get,
and what was more to be deplored, there was a lack of harmony.

But the need of a new house of worship, and in another
location, was now urgent. It was difficult to agree upon a
site. There is a tradition that at one time it was voted to
build upon the plain a little south of the present Post-Office,
and that "the people in Kent, who would not go furth,er
north, consented to go thus far from the old Meeting-House;
but at a subsequent meeting it was voted to build where the
house now stands." It was a bold step to remove so far.
There was then no other Church in what is now the town of
Wilton. Had the new house been placed south of the Post-
Office, and the road opened which now crosses the river near
the railroad station, it is quite possible that the ecclesiastical
history of Wilton for the last seventy-five years had been in
some respects different.

Timber, so far as it could be useful, was taken from the

---

* April 2d, 1789, voted to call Mr. Calvin White—yeas, 14; nays, 2. May 21st, 1792,
voted to call Mr. James Glassbrook to the work of the Ministry. Mr. Glassbrook
preached about a year at Salisbury, and died October, 1793. April 29th, 1793, voted to
call Mr. Methusaleh Bolding; 2 nays. In 1793, Rev. James Richards—a native of New
Canaan, and afterwards for many years a honored Professor in the Seminary at
Auburn—supplied the pulpit several Sabbaths.

old house to build the new,* which was erected A.D. 1790. The pulpit and seats of the old house were transferred to the new, and were used thirteen years, when new ones were substituted, which remained till 1844. The older persons present remember those seats: square pews under each gallery and one between the north corner pews, and the "great pew" which surrounded the pulpit as a court, and was the successor of the old times "deacons' seat." It was entered by two doors, between which, directly in front of the pulpit, was a shelf or narrow table that was transformed into the Communion-table by raising a leaf attached by hinges to the inner edge. This, when in position, was supported by an iron rod. The table and leaf were stained to imitate mahogany. The slips in the body of the house had a door at each end, as there were three aisles. The ceiling was arched. The galleries on each side, supported by four large pillars, were high, as was also the pulpit, which had its lofty, conical, but well-proportioned and ornamented sounding-board, firmly supported by two pillars that rose from the rear of the pulpit. The box of the pulpit was reached by a flight of stairs with balusters on either side, but when reached could with difficulty accommodate two persons.

The pew of the Pastor adjoined the great pew on the east side. Consequently, his family were under the constant inspection of the congregation. It might have been irksome to some of his children, but I do not remember that any person ever complained that they were not patterns of good behavior to other young people. †

This building was formally dedicated to Almighty God, in December, 1790. The sermon was preached, as is well remembered, though those who heard it have probably all departed this life, by Rev. Timothy Dwight, D. D., the al-

---

* The stones and underpinning of the old house were devoted to fencing the burying-ground where it stood. The vote to build was passed December 28th, 1789. The dimensions are fifty-four feet in length, forty feet in breadth, posts twenty-four feet in height.

† Outside, high up on the north side of the house, was painted on the siding what seemed, to near-sighted persons, a large window; but whose chief value to some irreverent boys on a week day was as a target for stones. They evidently did not apprehend the architectural fitness of the thing, and felt for it a boy's natural antipathy to shams.

ready distinguished Pastor of the Church on Greenfield Hill, and forever illustrious as the President of Yale College for nearly twenty-two years, from 1795 to 1817. His text was Genesis, 28 : 17, "How dreadful is this place! This is none other but the house of God, and this is the gate of heaven." Dr. Dwight's commendation of the house is remembered to this day.

Nearly three years afterwards, November 18, 1793, the Society, by a unanimous vote, invited to the pastorate Mr. AARON WOODWARD, at "a yearly salary of £100 lawful money, twenty cords of good wood, and the use of £150 until a parsonage shall be purchased." The experience of fixing the salary every year, at the end of the year, had not been pleasing. Mr. Woodward accepted the call, and was ordained Pastor the 8th of January, 1794. The ordination sermon was preached from Acts 26 : 18, by Rev. Benjamin Trumbull, D. D., Pastor in North Haven sixty years, from 1760 to 1820, and distinguished as the author of a valuable History of Connecticut.*

Mr. Woodward was born at North Coventry, Connecticut, October 14th, 1760, fitted for College with Rev. Nathan Williams, D. D., of Tolland, and Rev. Charles Backus, D. D., of Somers, graduated at Yale, September, 1789 ; studied Divinity with Dr. Trumbull, was licensed to preach by North Haven West Association, May 25, 1790. Theological Seminaries with a three years' course did not exist. Mr. Woodward had • received several invitations to settle before coming here. A little more than two weeks after his ordination he was married, January 24th, to Martha, eldest daughter of Dr. Trumbull. He brought his bride to Wilton on horseback, the approved method of travelling then, when one horse wagons and gigs were hardly known. For a time he lived in a part of Mr. Nathan Davenport's house, and afterwards built the one on the opposite side of the street, now owned by Mr.

---

* Other members of the Council were: Rev. Moses Mather, D. D., Thaddeus Bill, Middlesex (Darien); Rev. Hezekiah Ripley, Joseph Hyde, Greensfarms; Rev. Isaac Lewis, D.D., Dea. A. Mead, W. Greenwich; Rev. William Seward, Dea. I. Warren. Stanwich; Rev. Matthias Burnett, Dea. Thaddeus Betts, Norwalk ; Rev. Justus Mitchell, Dea. John Benedict (New) Canaan; Rev. John Noyes, Weston; John Taylor, Ridgebury; Rev. Samuel Goodrich, Dea. Nathan Olmstead, Ridgefield ; Rev. Daniel Smith, Dea. Silas Davenport, Stamford; Dea. Reuben Scofield, North Stamford.

William Sturges.* The record of baptisms shows three daughters born to Mr. Woodward while he resided in Wilton ; Martha Trumbull, baptized June 28th, 1795 ; Julia Ann, July, 1798 ; Jerusha, January, 1801. The catalogue shows that thirty-three, some of whom became very useful members,† were added to the Church, and one hundred and four baptized during the Ministry of Mr. Woodward. He probably left Wilton in the Spring of 1801. ‡ His health was, as it proved, permanently impaired, so that he was never able to resume the pastoral office, which he greatly loved. He bought a farm on the high lands of Wilbraham, Mass.,§ was for many years a Deacon in the Congregational Church there, and honored as one of its most valuable members. He had a strong voice, was fluent and very animated in conversation, easy in manner but decided in opinion. Says a gentlemen who knew him, ‖ " His many virtues, his sterling principles, his unswerving integrity, his devoted piety, are deeply engraven on my memory." Mr. Woodward died February 25th, 1840. Mrs. Woodward survived till December 10, 1851.

Rev. JOHN J. CARLE, a native of New Jersey, a graduate of Queen's, now Rutger's College, in 1789, who received the degree of A. M. from Princeton in 1792, was the next Pastor.¶

March 12th, 1801, the Society invited him to preach longer. Some circumstances, precisely what, does not appear, occasioned Mr. Carle to preach, on the 6th of April, a sermon before Rev. Messrs. Justus Mitchell, of New Canaan, Samuel Goodrich, of Ridgefield, and John Noyes of Weston.** These Ministers

---

* It used to be said that Mrs. Woodward's carpet was the first seen at Wilton, and was significant of other things.

† Among these may be mentioned Jonathan Middlebrook, afterwards Deacon, and a liberal donor to the fund. Nathan Hubbell, father of Rev. Stephen and Dea. Wakeman Hubbell, and Moses Gregory, father of Dea. Giles Gregory, of Wilton, and Dea. Ira Gregory, of Norwalk.

‡ As some compensation for his loss in going away, the Society voted, 27th Feb., 1800, his salary for the remainder of the year. When he ceased to supply the pulpit does not appear ; possibly in the Winter of 1801. But the Consociation to dismiss him probably met in the Spring of 1800.

§Letter of his daughter, Miss Jerusha Woodward, Wilbraham, Mass., under date of June 7th, 1876, from which much of the above is taken.

Benjamin C. Eastman, of New Haven.

¶Was Joseph Carle, one of the petitioners for Wilton Parish in 1726, an ancestor of Rev. John J. Carle ?

** Mr. Noyes was long known and loved in Wilton and elsewhere. He was a half-brother of Prof. Benjamin Silliman, Sr., and died 1846.

had been invited to hear him and advise with the Church and
Society "respecting the propriety of giving Mr. Carle a call at
the present time." Apparently these Ministers were not en-
tirely satisfied, and yet not fully persuaded of Mr. Carle's un-
fitness for the Pastorate. Their decision was sufficiently del-
phic. They judged "it advisable for Mr. Carle and the Society
to seek after further acquaintance." Thereupon the Society on
the same day unanimously requested Mr. Carle "to preach
longer," and three weeks later, with unanimity, called him to the
Pastorate. There is no allusion to the Church in these votes.
Perhaps the true office of the Society as the Trustee of the
property of the Church was not so well understood
as now. The salary offered was three hundred dollars
with the use of the land and buildings * owned by the
Society. Mr. Carle was installed June 3d, 1801. Three
years later he asked a dismission. There were reports
respecting his habits of drinking, it is said, which led
the Consociation to decline at that time to dismiss
him. Thereupon he publicly demitted the office of the Ministry, in the presence of the Council, giving emphasis to his
declaration by pulling off his coat. The tradition is that he
shortly returned to New Jersey, and died early, a victim of
intemperance. But I have found no authentic record of his
subsequent life.†

During the Pastorate of Mr. Carle, the parish of Wilton
was, A. D., 1802, incorporated by the Legislature into a town.
On the first of July of that year, members of St. Paul's Parish in
Norwalk, residing in Wilton, formed an Ecclesiastical Society
for the Protestant Episcopal Church known as St. Matthew's.‡

---

* Those purchased of Mr. Woodward.

† John H. Carle graduated at Rutger's in 1811, and preached at Marbletown, Hurley,
Shokan, Mapletown, and Currytown, N. J. Was he the son of John J. Carle?

‡ The meeting to organize this Society was, as the law direct d, called by the civil
authority, and held in the School-house at Pimpewaug. Samuel Belden was chosen
Moderator, David Lambert, Clerk, Daniel Church and Samuel Belden, Wardens. A
House of Worship was erected (38 feet by 28 feet), completed in 1803, and consecrated by Bishop Hobart. About sixteen years after, wings were added. A few years
since the present building of stone was erected in its place. The ground for the Ceme-
tery was the gift of John James Lambert, A. D., 1815. Three Methodist Episcopal
Churches have been buil't in Wilton, namely, at Bald Hill, Zion's Hill and Kent. Two
others are near the borders of the town one in Poplar Plain, the other in Georgetown.
A Protestant Methodist Church in Georgetown, organized about thirty-five years ago,
became a Congregatio al Church, June 15, 1875. It has nearly ninety members. Albert
H. Thompson is its Minister.

It is worthy of note in this connection as illustrating the liberality of the Congregationalists towards other denominations, that in 1758, James Truesdale was, by vote, " excused from paying a rate to the minister in case he get a certificate from the Baptist Society." In January, 1764, it was voted to abate the minister's rate to Mr. Whelpley "so long as he attends the Baptist meeting and no longer." In 1772 this Ecclesiastical Society began yearly to appoint a Special Collector * to take the Minister's rate from those living in the bounds of this Society, who belonged to St. Paul's Parish, and pay it to the Rector thereof, in the same manner as the others collected and paid over to their own Pastor the rates of other inhabitants. How rigidly the tax was collected may be inferred from one example. December 1st, 1730, Clapp Raymond, Justice of the Peace, notifies Abijah Betts that he is appointed Collector of the Society tax for the support of the Ministry, or, in default of payment, to levy on the goods of the delinquents, or in default of goods, to take their bodies to the jail in New Haven.

The next Pastor was SAMUEL FISHER. Mr. Fisher was born in Sunderland, Mass., the 3d of June, 1777. Three months before his birth, his father, who was an officer in the Continental army, had died at Morristown, New Jersey, where the main body of the army were in winter quarters, He graduated A. D., 1799, with the fifth class that completed its studies at Williams College.

He studied for the ministry with Rev. Dr. Hyde of Lee, Massachusetts, and before accepting a call to this Church, was ordained an Evangelist in October, A. D., 1805. Two months later, December 3d, 1805, he was installed as Pastor of the Church. In this office he enjoyed the lasting respect and esteem of many. His dismission occurred July 5th, 1809, that he might accept a call to Morristown, New Jersey,† where he was installed on the 9th of August following. Five years later he was called to the Presbyterian

---

* In various years Samuel Belden, David Lambert, Jr., Joseph P. Fitch and David Hurlbutt, were thus appointed.

† His predecessor at Morristown was the Rev. James Richards, D. D., already mentioned, who was that year called to Newark, N. J.

Church, in Patterson, where he labored twenty years. From that time his ministry was in different Churches, as Evangelist, or acting-Pastor. For five or six years he preached in Greenbush, opposite Albany. In 1837 he was chosen Moderator of the General Assembly of the Presbyterian Church, New School. Ten years before, in 1827, he received the degree of D. D., from Princeton College. One of the letters in Sprague's Annals was written by him, and gives a pleasant impression of his style of thought and expression. For a number of his later years he resided in Albany, in the family of his son, Rev. Samuel W. Fisher, D. D., who was born after the father left Wilton, became President of Hamilton College, and died a few years since. His own death occurred at Suckasunny, Morris County, New Jersey, the 27th of December, 1856, when he was in his eightieth year. Mr. Fisher's Ministry was valuable to the congregation. The evil effects of restoring the Half-Way Covenant, which for twenty years seem to have lingered in the Church, were partially tided over soon after his installation, by the adoption of the present Confession of Faith and Covenant. The seventy-three Communicants which he found were increased by forty-three during the less than five years of his Pastorate. In the year 1808, the last full year of his stay, twenty-six united with the Church. Possibly he would have remained longer as Pastor, except for the coldness produced towards him in some minds on account of his influence in securing the giving up of the Half-Way Covenant. But the interests of the kingdom of Christ and the spiritual blessings, which, in the next twenty-five years, increased the Church two or three fold, is a sufficient justification of the wisdom of his course.

The next year after the dismission of Mr. Fisher, October 17th, 1810, Rev. SYLVANUS HAIGHT was installed. Mr. Haight was born at Fishkill, New York, July 22d, 1776, almost one hundred years ago. He entered Union College, Oct. 7, 1797, in the class of 1801, and remained till the Spring of 1800. There he distinguished himself as a speaker. He preached as an evangelist in several places in the State of New York, and came here from Galway, Saratoga County, where his ministrations had been especially blessed. He entered most heartily into his work here, and for several reasons that period in which he was Pastor, was memorable in the history of the Church. The era of revivals had fairly begun. This Church, especially for the first thirteen years of Mr. Haight's pastorate, profited by them. In 1816 and again in 1822 a large number was added to the Church. About one hundred and sixty were received to the Church during his pastorate of nearly twenty-one years.

The salary paid by the Society had always been small, and as the tide of emigration had fairly begun to flow, was not likely to be larger. Other Churches were raising funds; the better to secure themselves against the evils of poverty, and against the mischief which was threatened, when the salary must be raised by other means than taxation. It was resolved to make the attempt here. Matthew Marvin, Esq., and Mr. Haight were the leaders in the work. The subscription was commenced January 1st, 1813, the condition being that unless four thousand dollars were pledged, no subscriber should be bound. After no little effort it lacked sixteen dollars of the required sum. Mr. Haight who had already agreed to make an annual deduction of fifty dollars from his salary, subscribed the sixteen dollars in the name of a stranger.* Subsequently, Samuel Middlebrook and Jonathan Middlebrook, left each a legacy of five hundred dollars to remain on interest till the amount should be a thousand dollars. The two thousand thus secured were added to the fund increasing it to six thousand dollars. The payment of the several subscriptions to the Society was made sure by "Esquire Marvin," who advanced the money and received the notes of the subscribers payable to himself. From 1812 to his death in 1842, he was the Treasurer of the Society. Since that time his mantle has rested upon his son, Deacon Charles Marvin.† Before the settlement of Mr. Haight, the Society owned a parsonage which was built by Mr. Woodward. Mr. Haight pre-

---

* Prominent among the donors were, Matthew Marvin ($650), Samuel Comstock and Strong Comstock and Mary Betts, each $200.

† Previous to 1790, for many years Abijah Betts was Treasurer, and from 1790 to 1812, Major Samuel Comstock.

vailed upon the Society to sell, and paid twenty-seven hundred dollars for it, which sum was added to the fund. In 1832-3 the present parsonage was built. The principal of the fund has, in various ways increased, till, with the Parsonage property, it amounts to ten thousand dollars, which affords a reasonable assurance that this Church will not need aid from the Connecticut Home Missionary Society for a long time to come, and also binds those who enjoy these fruits of the self-sacrifice and wise forethought of the Christian men and women who have gone before us, to remember generously those churches in this State and elsewhere that have fallen into poverty.

Another important event of Mr. Haight's ministry was the opening of the Wilton Academy. HAWLEY OLMSTEAD--a man worthy to be held in lasting remembrance—graduated at Yale College the foremost scholar of the Class of 1816.* He designed to study law, but a failure of his eyes in college induced him to open a school as an experiment. Dartmouth College had its origin in a small school building yet standing in Columbia, Connecticut. The Wilton Academy was opened in 1816 in a small building, afterwards for many years used by the late Nathan Comstock as a store. It was soon seen that the young teacher had rare gifts for his office. Before entering College he had taught a district school and, as assistant pupil, had aided Rev. William Belden—himself a Wilton man—at that time Pastor in Greenfield and Principal of its Academy. An Academy building was erected in 1820.†

---

* Hawley Olmstead, son of Aaron and Sarah Esther (Hawley) Olmstead, born Dec. 17th, 1793, was descended on his father's side from Richard Olmstead, one of the first settlers of Norwalk, and its first Representative in the Colonial Legislature. His mother was a "great-granddaughter" of Rev. Thomas Hawley, of Northampton, Mass., who was a graduate of Harvard College in 1709 and the first minister of Ridgefield, Conn. Mr. Olmstead married Miss Harriet Smith, of New Canaan, a niece of Rev. Daniel Smith, who was fifty-three years (1793-1846) Pastor of the First Church, Stamford. Mrs. Olmstead still resides in New Haven.

† The land upon which the Academy was built was given "for the advancement of literature and science, and especially for the good will I have and bear to the Presbyterian Society of Wilton" by Nathan Comstock, to "David Willard, Samuel Comstock, 2d, and Lewis Gregory—Committee of the Presbyterian Society of Wilton—for the time being, and to their successors in office forever." The land given was sixty-five feet front, and seventy deep. The land was to be used only for the erection of a building or buildings for "a school of higher order, and for religious and singing meetings," "which school, kept in said house, is to be under the direction of the Clergyman of the Presbyterian Society, for the time being, and his successors in office, and the Preceptor of the school; and in case of the Society's being vacant or destitute of a Clergyman, to be under the direction of the Committee of said Society." The date of the deed is March 25th, 1820. Mention is made that the school at that time was in Mr. Comstock's store. The witnesses are Sylvanus Haight and Matthew Marvin. The deed is acknowledged before Matthew Marvin, Justice of the Peace, and is evidently in his handwriting.

It stood south of the road, between the present site of the Town House and the Parsonage. About the year 1832 it was removed to a spot a little northeast of the present Chapel. The old building was sold, about 1870, to William A. Sturges, and stands near the Post-Office. Mr. Haight, with his usual enthusiasm, aided to publish the excellencies of the teacher and to procure pupils from abroad. The two first pupils fitted here for College—Nathaniel Bouton and Jared B. Waterbury—have long been among the most honored and useful ministers of their generation. Each received the degree of D.D. many years since. Dr. Bouton, for forty years Pastor of the Church in Concord, New Hampshire, is recognized as the Historian of that State. The school so prospered that after four and a half years Mr. Olmstead was persuaded to remove to Norwalk. His health became impaired, and three years later he returned to Wilton to rest and engage in agriculture. He also heard private pupils. At the end of two and a half years, in 1826, he again opened his school, at first in the Academy, and when the Town Hall was built, a few years after, in the upper room of that building. There he continued thirteen years, with no public examination, no private circulars, no advertisement, and yet uniformly a full attendance of pupils. When he left Wilton, in 1839, to become Rector of the Hopkins' Grammar School, in New Haven —an institution forty years older than the College—he had had pupils from nearly, or quite, every State in the Union, and from several foreign countries. Some of the Christian young men, whose names are yet held in loving remembrance here, had made themselves very useful in the Sabbath school and in social religious meetings.*

After ten years of extraordinary success in the Grammar School, Mr. Olmstead's health failed and he relinquished the rectorship to his son, who had for two years been his assistant. For ten years longer he taught private pupils in his own house. In 1862 he received from Yale the degree of

---

* Among these Lockwood, David P. Judson, Stiles Hawley, James Smith, Nathaniel Wade, Willis Lord, E. B. Clark, Benjamin Smith, Ira Lawton, Edward Strong, Amos Cook, and Myron N. Morris.

LL.D.   His death occurred the 3d of December, 1868, while he was addressing, in his own parlor, a club of ministers and laymen, with whom for more than twenty years he had met weekly to discuss some great moral and religious questions. Said an eye-witness: " He had just completed a most thorough, logical, and, as his companions felt, richly beautiful argument.   It was, indeed, the beautful death of the Christian soldier with his armor on, the disciple going out of the earthly service to the ' well done' of his Lord."

In one of the later years of his life, anticipating some such day as this for Wilton, and thinking he might not be present, Mr. Olmstead charged me to give a sentiment, which will be recognized as characteristic of the man, and is fit to be engraven as his epitaph.   It was this: " *Unswerving, supreme fidelity to Truth and Right.*"*

Happily for Wilton the health of Mr. Edward Olmstead, who was for two years the assistant and then the successor of his father in the Hopkins' Grammar School, became impaired after a few years, which eventually occasioned his return to Wilton in 1855 to resume the work of the Academy; at first in the room vacated by Mr. Hawley Olmstead in 1839, and afterwards in a building of his own, where he continues to this day doing for the children what his honored father had done for their parents.

One fact connected with the Academy ought to be mentioned.   Though it has done so much for Wilton, it has no funds, and beyond the room rent of the old Academy and the room over the Town Hall, has received no gratuitous pecuniary aid from the town, the Ecclesiastical Society, or individuals.   If some who have shared its advantages, with benevolent desire that others might receive like benefits, would provide a generous endowment, they might sow seed that would bear fruit of inestimable value when they have gone to their reward.

* Mr. Olmstead was of med um height, stoutly built, very erect, and dignified in his carriage, but courteous and affable in his address. He governed his school and won the lasting respect of his pupils in a remarkable degree with little apparent effort. His interest in Wilton was deep and constant to the day of his death. He was a member of the Legislature in 1825, '26. '28 and '29. and a Senator from New Haven in 1853. As Chairman of the Committee on Education in 1825, and again in 1828, he presented reports on Common School Education that attracted much attention and exercised a lasting influence.

When Mr. Haight was ordained there were few buildings of any kind near the Meeting-House, except the one nearest to it on the east, recently occupied by Mr. Moses Betts. There was no house on the road towards Kent till one reached that now occupied by Mr. John Betts near the river. The house of Dea. Daniel Gregory on the hill, west, now occupied by his grandson, William D. Gregory, was the only one near this house except the one across the bridge on the north, now the residence of Dea. Edward Olmstead. There was here no parsonage, no town house, conference room, or horse sheds. If in remote parts of the town dwellings have decreased, there has been growth in this neighborhood. The Academy and the opening of the railroad in 1852 have contributed to this.

The great temperance revival of this century began while Mr. Haight was Pastor, and he threw himself into it early in his ministry with characteristic ardor. There has been a change in the drinking habits of the people which the young people can hardly realize. So late as 1829, the Temperance Reformation, which then only discarded distilled liquors, had gained such headway that one man determined, without the aid of alcoholic liquor, to raise his barn, which stands near here; but so many men refused to complete the raising that he was obliged to send for strong drink. A few weeks later another man put up the frame of a barn in Kent, supplying nothing stronger than ale. This was said to be the first large building in town raised without the help of distilled liquor.

The energy, zeal, and earnestness in the work of the ministry which characterized Mr. Haight were remarkable. His sympathy with his friends in their affliction, and his readiness to make personal sacrifice for their advantage, were extraordinary. Perhaps a greater prudence in speech, when silence had been golden, had enabled him longer to escape some of the unfriendliness that clouded the later years of his ministry, and to the great sorrow of many who never cease to love him, and to his own great affliction, led to his dismission August 17th, 1831. In the Spring of 1832, having sold his residence in Kent, since occupied by the family of Erastus Sturges, he removed to Pottsville, Pennsylvania, in which and in Norriton, Port Carbon, and other places, his ministry was highly successful.   In 1846 he was, at the age of seventy years, installed Pastor at Bethel.   Afterwards he resided in Wilton, supplying neighboring Churches for a longer or shorter period, where his ministrations were very acceptable. In 1849 he removed to South Norwalk, where he preached three years (1848–1851).   As opportunity offered, he continued his loved employment till within a few weeks of his death, which occurred April 6th, 1864, in the eighty-eighth year of his age.   He was buried, at his own request, in Greensfarms, because he would be in death near his venerated friend, Rev. Hezekiah Ripley, D.D., who was fifty-four years Pastor of the Church in that place.

Perhaps I cannot better conclude this sketch of Mr. Haight than by quoting from an article published after his decease* by the Secretary of the New York State Medical Society,† who was born and reared in Wilton.   He says: "Mr. Haight was a man of quick impulses and ponderous energy.   His will seemed to me inflexible, and he moved with impetuous force for its accomplishment.   His person was massive, his head large, and his skin bronzed.   When in after years I saw and heard Daniel Webster, I was greatly impressed with a similarity between them.   Not that they were alike.   Mr. Webster's movements were slow and majestic, but there was the massive body, the large head, and the bronzed face. Both were eloquent.   Mr. Webster was calm, majestic, logical; Mr. Haight bold, powerful, impassioned.   He would have been a prominent man had he been thrown into political life.   His courage, his daring, his enterprise would have commended him to Napoleon as worthy of one of his Generals.

"I remember the beautiful summer afternoon in August, 1831, when a mere child, I went with my father to hear his farewell sermon.   He was in the lofty pulpit of the old Church, which was very high and seemed to my childish eyes a great deal higher than it really was.   In it his figure

---

* "Norwalk Gazette," May 3d, 1864.

† Sylvester Willard, M.D., born June 19, 1825; died at Albany, April 2d, 1865.

rose majestically. His powerful voice was melted in tenderness. The scenes of joy and sorrow through which he had passed with that people seemed to pass before him anew. When he concluded his sermon the people wept; his heart was swollen with emotion, and his voice faltered, but with immense power and solemnity he concluded: 'Amen! and amen to this Bible,' at the same time laying his hand with heavy emphasis upon it. I was frightened, and thought the world was coming to an end. On my way home, I remember, I asked my father if there were to be no more Sundays! He replied: 'Yes, but Mr. Haight was not to be our Minister any longer.'"*

In December, 1831, Rev. SAMUEL MERWIN—a native of Milford, a graduate of Yale in 1802—took a dismission from the North Church in New Haven, of which he had been Pastor nearly twenty-seven years, and to which, during his ministry, eight hundred and fifty persons were added. He accepted a call to this Church, and on the 23d of February, 1832 (ninety-nine years after the ordination of Mr. Gaylord), was installed its Pastor.† A few months after Mr. Merwin's settlement a deep religious interest was manifest, and Mr. Nettleton, who, for twenty-five years or more, had been distinguished as an Evangelist, aided him awhile. Several were added to the Church that year, and some each succeeding year, but most in 1836. The whole number received to the Church during Mr. Merwin's ministry was fifty. In a variety of ways his pastorate was valuable to the people. They needed to be especially instructed in the doctrines of the Bible. They were, unhappily, divided by the events of the few preceding years, and Mr. Merwin's large experience, eminent prudence,

---

* Mr. Haight was twice married. The children of his first wife were Martha, Clarissa, Sylvanus, Frances and Henry—three daughters and two sons. Both the sons and the youngest daughter, as I remember, died before their father. The second Mrs. Haight—formerly Mrs. Brush, a very estimable woman—died in Norwalk a few years since.

† The members of the Councils which ordained Messrs. Carle, Fisher and Haight are not named on the Church record. At Mr. Merwin's installation there were present: Rev. Daniel Smith, Stamford; Rev. Platt Buffett, Dea. E. Close, Stanwich; Rev. Joel Mann, Isaac Holley, West Greenwich; Rev. Henry Fuller, William Crissy, North Stamford; Rev. Ebenezer Platt, Joseph Mather, Darien; Rev. John H. Hunter, Charles Bennett, Fairfield; Rev. Chauncey Wilcox, Dea. Obadiah Mead, North Greenwich; Rev. Nathaniel Hewitt, D.D., Jesse Sterling, Bridgeport; Rev. Charles G. Selleck, Dea. Harvey Smith, Ridgefield; Dea. Seth Hickok, New Canaan; Deacon Hyde, Greensfarms; Benjamin Lynes, Ridgebury; Daniel K. Nash, Norwalk.

and clearly arranged sermons tended to enlighten the conscience, to produce harmony, and to elevate the standard of religious life. And it might be added, if this were the two hundredth anniversary of the foundation of this Church, that his family—of which Mrs. Merwin was the pattern, and with her husband the head, bringing with them the culture of a lifetime in New Haven—exerted, unconsciously perhaps, a refining and healthful influence upon many households. It is significant, that the first young lady to recite in Latin in the Wilton Academy was a daughter of Mr. Merwin.

The health of Mr. Merwin had been impaired by the amount of labor incident to the large numbers gathered into the New Haven Church during his ministry. As years went on it did not improve in Wilton, and he asked for a dismission. The Church at first opposed, but consented to call the Consociation, and the pastoral relation was dissolved the 25th of September, 1838. Mr. Merwin removed to New Haven, and, though not again undertaking a pastoral charge, was active in Christian work in various ways; was helpful as a member of occasional Councils; was often consulted in Ecclesiastical matters, and enjoyed in a high degree the respect and confidence of the Christian public. His pleasure in the study of the Word of God seemed to increase as the years went on. He was remarkably gifted in prayer, in which the words of the inspired writers were continually quoted with surprising facility and aptness. It was his joy in the declining years of his life "to visit the afflicted with Christian consolation, to pray by the bedside of the sick or dying, and to preach the Gospel to the poor." His custom on the Sabbath was to conduct a religious service in the Chapel of the Almshouse.

On the 25th of February, 1855, he preached a semi-centennial sermon in the North Church, commemorative of his pastorate there and in Wilton. This (at the request of Governor Dutton, James Brewster and others) was published, and, happily, prefaced with an excellent likeness of Mr. Merwin. On the 22d of October the same year, Mr. and Mrs. Merwin and their two sons and five daughters, with their sons-in-law and daughters-in-law (six ministers in all and eight graduates, the family having lost none by death), celebrated their golden wedding amid the congratulations of many friends. Before another year, on the 3d of September, 1856, Mr. Merwin departed this life.

In preaching at his funeral Dr. Bacon said :* "The close of his life was in perfect harmony with its course. Paralysis had impaired his physical strength, and to some extent the clearness of his memory and the activity of his mental powers, yet life had not become a burden; and while he knew that death was at the door, and was in daily expectation of the summons, he could enjoy, with a cheerful and grateful mind, the society and the assiduous attention of her with whom he had walked hand in hand for more than fifty years and of their children who gathered around him from their homes; and when he lay upon the bed from which he was to rise no more, while all the delights of earth and time were failing, he delighted still in prayer. At my last visit to him we had kneeled at his bedside to pray, and when the words from my lips were ended, his own voice took up the strains of supplication, and in his own tones, and his own characteristic style of utterance, with no fault of memory or connection, and with no iteration of petitions already offered, he led us again to the Throne of Grace. Thus, calmly, meekly, patiently, devoutly, he died, as he had lived, knowing in whom he had believed."†

During Mr. Merwin's ministry here, a great tempest of controversy raged in Connecticut, and elsewhere, on questions of religious doctrine, in which some of the members of Fairfield West Association were deeply interested, and the Churches much divided. The East Windsor (now Hartford) Theological Institute grew out of that discussion. Happily, Mr. Merwin, while holding decidedly to the theology he had learned from Dwight and Edwards, and in full sympathy

---

* Congregational Year Book, 1857, p. 119.

† Mr. Merwin was of medium stature and size, erect, active, and walked with elastic step. He had dark eyes, a benevolent countenance; in conversation was grave or cheerful, as occasion served; spoke with a deep, musical voice, and so well balanced was his judgment that he rarely gave utterance to words he would wish to recall.

with New Haven Divinity, as it was called, continued to preach as he had been accustomed to do before, and this Church was not agitated by that storm. After the dismission of Mr. Merwin numerous candidates were heard, of whom Rev. Henry Benedict, formerly Pastor four years in Norwalk* and, afterwards for twelve years acting-Pastor in Westport, received a call, which he declined.

On the 22d of February, 1839, Rev. JOHN SMITH was installed the ninth Pastor of this Church. Mr. Smith was a graduate of Yale College in 1821. He was born in Wethersfield, Ct., September 2d, 1796, the son of James and Sarah (Hanmer) Smith. He studied theology two years at Andover, and one year at Princeton, was licensed to preach by Fairfield East Association April 24th, 1824, and ordained Pastor of the Presbyterian Church in Trenton, New Jersey, on the 8th of March, 1826. This charge he resigned in August, 1828, and the 12th of March following (1829) was installed Pastor of the Congregational Church in Exeter, New Hampshire. After a pastorate of about nine years he was dismissed February 14th, 1838. After spending a portion of the year as an agent of the American Tract Society, he was installed here the 22d of February, 1839. Three years later occurred one of the most remarkable revivals in the history of the Church, as a result of which the second Sabbath in May, 1842, ninety-five were added to the Church, ninety-three or four by profession, about half of whom were baptized at that time. Mr. Smith had some excellent gifts for pastoral work, in which he was untiring. He was interested in the schools, and a portion of the time School Visitor. His presence was understood to be welcome in neighboring Churches when he exchanged. Without being showy his sermons were sound in doctrine, and furnished food for profitable thought. He was a man of peace, and spiritually minded. His conduct and conversation tended to promote unity and brotherly love. Above one hundred and thirty were received to the Church during his ministry.

---

* 1828–1832.

Next to the revival of 1842 the event of his ministry was the remodeling of the Church edifice. At its annual meeting, about the beginning of the year 1844, the Society voted to remove the sounding-board from above the pulpit. Before the meeting adjourned, a member* who was expert in the use of tools had appointed himself a Committee, procured a saw, and carried the vote into execution. But now the crowning glory of the house was gone. The need of doing more was painfully apparent. A movement was soon made, in which the present Senior Deacon was foremost, to raise a fund, lower the galleries, reseat the house, build a new pulpit, and to make such other changes within and without as convenience and taste required. Rarely has an undertaking to modernize an old house been more successful. While the work was in progress the usual Sabbath services were held in the Conference room. Most of those who were active in this work—men and women honored and beloved, and especially dear to many who are here—sleep with their fathers, who built the house fifty-five years earlier. Others yet survive to enjoy, with a younger generation, the fruit of their labors and gifts for the house of the Lord.†

In 1848 Mr. Smith asked a dismission. Action in calling Consociation was delayed several months. He was dismissed in June. On the 26th of July, 1848, he was installed Pastor in Kingston, New Hampshire, where he remained till early in the year 1855. Removing to Stamford, Conn., he preached about two years (1856–1858) in Long Ridge and occasionally elsewhere. He continued to reside in Stamford with his sons —who were successful merchants in New York—till his death, from pneumonia, the 20th of February, 1874, in his seventy-eighth year.

Mr. Smith was married September 11th, 1826, to Miss Esther Mary Woodruff, daughter of Hon. Dickinson Woodruff, of Trenton, N. J. About a year after his settlement here she suddenly died, leaving him with six children,‡ the

---

* Mr. Henry G. Middlebrook.

† A Fair was held to aid in procuring furniture. See Appendix.

‡ Their names were Susan, James D., Charles, Esther, Walter, and Maria.

youngest a daughter, whose eyes first opened to the light a few hours before. The grave of Mrs. Smith is with the mothers' and daughters' of this people; but that great sorrow cast a shadow over all his subsequent life in Wilton. In 1843 he married Miss Louisa Gridley, of Middletown, now Cromwell, who died (without children) some time before her husband.

When Mr. Smith was dismissed, there was in the Divinity School at New Haven, and in the College Faculty as Tutor, a young man, who had graduated five years before, at Yale, with the highest honor; who was born in India, and bore the name of his father, who was one of those godly men that prayed at Williams for the heathen, and petitioned the General Association of Massachusetts to aid the young men who desired to go and preach to the heathen, and who, when having reached Calcutta, and having been refused permission to stay in India, with his associates, so wisely and vigorously reasoned with the authorities, that, after a protracted and painful struggle, consent was obtained, and he remained a "wise, intrepid, patient, self-sacrificing missionary" till, in 1826, while on a journey, having been attacked by the cholera, lying on the veranda of a heathen temple, GORDON HALL breathed out his life with the thrice repeated words: "Glory to Thee, O God." The son, with his mother, Mrs. Margaret (Lewis) Hall, reached this country a little before his father's death. It happened that two of his College classmates* were natives of Wilton, one of whom was also a Tutor at that time. Mr. Hall, after preaching a few Sabbaths, received a call to the pastorate. October 10th he was married to Miss Emily, youngest daughter of Rev. Samuel Merwin, and on the 25th of October, 1848—a little more than ten years after Mr. Merwin's dismission—Mr. Hall was ordained Pastor. The pastorate continued till the 4th of May, 1852, when he was dismissed, that he might accept a call to the Edwards Church, Northampton, Mass., over which he was installed a month later, the 2d of June, 1852. Mr. Hall's ministry in Wilton, though brief, was fruitful in addi-

---

* Lewis R. Hurlbutt, M.D., of Stamford, and Charles Jones, Esq., of New York.

tions to the Church and in the quickened lives of Christians. Sixty-six were added to the communicants. The blessing that attended his labors equalled the hopes of his friends. Had the Committee of the Edwards Church, whose report occasioned his call thither, heard some of the comments on their proceedings, they might have accepted them as evidence of their sagacity in choosing for their Pastor one from whom his people would not willingly part. In 1864 Mr. Hall received D. D. from Amherst College.

While all his predecessors in office in this Church, and his two immediate successors, are no longer on earth, happily, Dr. Hall yet lives, honored and beloved. And we may hope that when this Church, in the first year of the next century, shall celebrate its one hundred and seventy-fifth anniversary, or the Town its Centennial in 1902, he may be permitted to honor the occasion with his presence, and receive the congratulations of those who are then here, that he has celebrated his golden wedding.

It was the 6th of July, 1853, when the next Pastor, THOMAS SCOTT BRADLEY, was ordained. Mr. Bradley was born at Lee, Mass., the eldest son of Eli Bradley,* April 15th, 1825. His ancestors were God-fearing people, and he united with the Church, in Lee, at the age of sixteen. At twenty he entered Williams College, and graduated in 1848, with an honorable stand. Three years later, in the Class of 1851, he graduated at Andover Seminary. Next, he spent six months with Rev. John Todd, D.D., in Pittsfield, Mass., in parish work. He preached meantime in Lanesboro', Mass., and afterwards six months in Cornwall, Conn. Mr. Bradley was tall, strongly built, energetic, rapid in his movements, earnest in his convictions, and prudent in speech. He was a popular preacher, affable in conversation, and fond of practical matters; but the condition of his health did not encourage protracted application in the study, and, in 1857, he was dismissed at his own request.† For a

---

* Durfee's Annals of Williams College, p. 171.

* A sermon preached at the funeral of Mrs. Abby (Gregory) Willard, January, 1857, was published.

time he taught, with marked ability, the High School in
South Norwalk.   Afterwards he became Pastor in New
Lebanon, New York.   In 1862 he accepted a commission
of Captain in the Ninth Company of New York Sharp-
shooters, in which, through his influence, many of his young
men enlisted.   He was sent to Suffolk, Virginia, and, in
withstanding a siege and as skirmishers, the Company saw
much hard service.   Mr. Bradley's health failed from long
exposure in the trenches, and he set out on a furlough for the
North ; but at Philadelphia the typhoid fever prostrated him.
He greatly desired to reach home and see his friends once
more ; but that was not granted.   He telegraphed for Mrs.
Bradley, who came and did what she could, till on the 28th
of June, 1863, at the age of thirty-eight, he died.   His body
was buried by the side of his father in Lee.

Before coming to Wilton he married Miss Harriet L.
Reed, of Milan, Ohio, where he had for some time taught
a school.   They had two children—Samuel R. Bradley and
Hattie Bell Bradley—both living.   Mrs. Bradley returned to
her father's in Milan, and died with consumption.

The successor of Mr. Bradley in Wilton was CHARLES
BASSETT BALL, who was ordained here the 20th of January,
1858.   Mr. Ball* was a townsman of Mr. Bradley, having
been born in Lee, Mass., the 9th of July, 1825.   He was the
son of Isaac and Lydia Ball, and graduated at Williams in
the Class of 1846.   The condition of his health turned him
from the ministry, and he taught for some time in the pleasant
village of Southampton, L. I.   Then he studied law, and
practiced some years in Springfield, Mass.   The improvement
in his health led him to turn again to his early thought of
preaching the Gospel.   He studied theology for awhile at
East Windsor.   His call to this Church was by no means
unanimous,- but his excellent spirit, his desire for the con-
version of sinners, his skill in conversing with his parish-
ioners, his open-hearted friendliness, and the manifest divine
approval of his ministry, won the hearts of his people.   The

---

* Durfee's Annals, p. 561.

year was highly prosperous. Thirty-one were added to the Church by profession. At his death, which occurred suddenly, January 27th, 1859, in consequence of a malignant tumor near the lower jaw, there was universal lamentation. A delegation from the congregation carried his mortal remains to Lee for burial. He was in the thirty-fourth year of his age.

Before coming to Wilton he married Miss Sarah Huntting, of Southampton, Long Island, who is now Mrs. William J. Bartlett, of Lee, Mass. He left a daughter, Hattie S., born January, 1859.

In the October following Mr. Ball's decease, the Church called Rev. SAMUEL R. DIMOCK, who was installed December 7th, 1859. Mr. Dimock was a native of Coventry, Tolland County, Ct., born May 28, 1822, nurtured in Mansfield, a graduate with honor of Yale in the Class of 1847, a teacher of a private school for several years in Manchester, Conn. His first settlement was at Valentia, Kinderhook, N. Y. He was dismissed from Wilton, June 8th, 1861, and installed over the South Church, Pittsfield, Mass., the 24th of September the same year. Three years after he accepted a call to Syracuse, where he was installed the 14th of September, 1864. Taking a dismission from Syracuse, October 13th, 1868, his next parish was in Quincy, Illinois, in which he remained about two years. Thence he removed to Nebraska; first to Crete in 1871, then became Pastor in 1872 of the Church in Lincoln, where he was succeeded last year by one of our own townsmen,* whom we would gladly have with us to-day. In 1875 he became acting-Pastor of the Church in Central City, Colorado.

In 1849 Mr. Dimock was married to Miss Louisa S. Dimock, who died at Manchester in 1855. In 1858 he married Miss Anna S. Husted.

The successor of Mr. Dimock in the pastoral office here was the Rev. WHEELOCK NYE HARVEY, of Massachusetts stock, a native of Jamestown, Chatauque County, N. Y., born

---

* Rev. Lewis Gregory, Y C., 1864, grandson of Moses, and son of Charles and Harriet (Clark) Gregory.

April 15th, 1825, the son of Charles R. and Olive (Willard-Harvey, a graduate of the New York University in 1844. Mr. Harvey studied divinity at the Union Theological Seminary, New York, was ordained Pastor at Bethel, Conn., May 18th, 1853, where he remained about five years. October 24th, 1858, he began as Pastor elect to minister to the Second Church in Milford. He remained in that relation three years, when he received a call to Wilton, and was installed January 1st, 1862. The records of the Church show that his ministry here was profitable. Forty-seven were added to the Church, thirty of whom came by profession.

Mr. Harvey's health was so much impaired that, much to the regret of the Church, he felt the necessity of relief from pastoral labor. He was dismissed October 15th, 1867. He now resides in New York. A difficulty in hearing led him to relinquish the work of preaching, which he greatly loved, and go into business with his father.*

He married Miss Margaret Lewis, daughter of Edward and Cynthia (Gildersleeve) Lewis, of Portland, Conn., a graduate of Mount Holycke Seminary. They have four children: Alice, Lewis, Hattie and Charlie.

The fifteenth Pastor of this Church, Rev. SAMUEL J. M. MERWIN, was a graduate of Yale in the Class of 1839, ordained Pastor of the Church in Southport, December 18th, 1844, and was dismissed, at his own request, May 3d, 1859. After a season of rest he was installed over the Church at South Hadley Falls, Massachusetts, December 4th, 1860. The call to this Church, as successor to his father and brother, was accepted in 1868, and he was installed by the Consociation the 26th of October the same year. Happily, Mr. Merwin's ministry has not yet passed into history, and as the honored Pastor of the Church of which he was the foster son, with which he united by confession of faith above forty years ago, he has no need that another should speak for him to-day.

Among the memorable things of the last eight years is the

---

* A sermon preached by Mr. Harvey, on Thanksgiving Day, November, 1863, was published.

building of a new and commodious chapel, with conveniences for the work of the Ladies' Society attached; also, the introduction of a large and excellent organ. These are pleasing evidences that in material prosperity the Church and Society are not decaying, and that it is not altogether unmindful of the duties which its opportunities impose.

There are many topics, and many persons, who, to-day, should be remembered by us, as reverent and dutiful children. There are many whose names even are forgotten, and of whose individual lives we are ignorant, who worthily contributed to build not the material houses of worship only, but the spiritual walls of this Church. Though we pass them in silence they may well have our honor and gratitude sharing these with those we knew and loved, whom the time would fail to mention. Yet there are a few whom the Church honored by calling them to special service, which they rendered with alacrity and fidelity. These are the men, who used the office of Deacon well. Of these we have the names of twenty-two, but unhappily, for the first hundred years and more, there is, with few exceptions, no record of their election, and rarely one of their death. Apparently they died in office, except perhaps two or three who removed from the place.

The first three mentioned are *Benjamin Hickok*, *Jonathan Elmer* and *James Trowbridge*. These were probably original members of the Church, since they were a part of the Committee appointed by the Society to make arrangements for the settlement of Mr. Sturgeon.

Deacon Hickok is supposed to have left a son, Benjamin, who united with the Church by the Half-Way Covenant, with his wife, March 27, 1763, who was the father of Esther, the wife of Dea. Daniel Gregory, and lived to an advanced age.

The house of the son—perhaps of the father—stood near the spot occupied by the building now used for the Academy, and was torn down early in this century. " Benjamin Hickok, Esq.," who died the 17th of November, 1745, aged 59 years, was probably the Deacon.

Dea. *Jonathan Elmer* was chosen, before the Church had a

Pastor, to read the Psalm. As few had Psalm Books, we may understand that he read only one or two lines at a time, so that all who could, might sing the words. This was called "lining" and sometimes "deaconing" the hymn. There was an Eliakim Elmer, who lived near the Bridge on the Ridgefield Road in 1738; but Deacon Elmer's name does not, I believe, occur after 1746. Jonathan Elmer, probably a son of the Deacon, united with the Church in June, 1742.

Of Dea. *James Trowbridge* there is no information, and the name early disappears from the Church records. In New Canaan the name remains.

Dea. *Matthew Gregory*, was born in 1680. The place of his birth is not known. Some of his grandchildren believed that he came from England. He is supposed to have been in Wilton as early as 1718.* He had two sons, Ezra and Matthew; the latter known also as Ensign Matthew, who was the father of Dea. Daniel Gregory. He died in 1777, at the age of 97 years, the year following the death of his son Ezra. His wife Hannah had died ten years earlier. His son Matthew died October 30, 1756, aged 45 years. A well-worn path through the fields west of his house signified to his children his daily habit of secret communing with God.

Dea. *James Keeler* is not identified, except Feb. 18, 1759, James Keeler and wife were received to the Church on the Half-Way Covenant. When they became communicants is not stated.

Dea. *James Olmstead* is believed to have been the son of Samuel Olmstead. He had a son James who had a son Aaron, who was the father of Hawley Olmstead, LL.D. His name, with that of Mary his wife, occurs on the Church records as admitted by the Half-Way Covenant, Feb. 22, 1756. In 1776 he is called Deacon Olmstead. On a stone of gray marble in the old burying-ground, we read that he died March 17, 1777, aged 68 years.

Dea. *Nathan Comstock* is first mentioned as Deacon, Dec. 15,

* His letter to the Church was brought from Norwalk, 1740. His house was a few rods north of that builded about 1740 for his son Ezra, in which his grandson Moses lived, and his great-granddaughter, Miss Clara M. Gregory, now resides.

1766. Among those married by Mr. Gaylord, are (March 7, 1738-9) Nathan Comstock and Bethiah Strong. In 1740, he united with the Church. Major Samuel Comstock and Strong Comstock, the father of Samuel, Edward, William and Nathan, were his children. His residence was probably the house in which his grandchildren, Edward and Polly Comstock, lived, a little west of the road from Belden's Hill to Ridgefield, near its junction with the Ridgefield road.

Dea. *Nathan Hubbell.*—In May, 1747, there came by letter from Greenfield three men with their wives and the wife of a fourth, who was a son of one of the three. One of these couples was Nathan Hubbell and Martha, his wife. Eight years later, December 2, 1755, Mrs. Hubbell, the wife of Nathan, died, aged 53 years; and 1761, Feb. 6, Nathan Hubbell died, aged 61 years. Three years later, June 17, 1764, Capt. Nathan Hubbell was received to the Church. In the absence of evidence to the contrary, it is easy to believe that he was the son of the afore-mentioned Nathan Hubbell. He became Deacon Hubbell, Aug. 23, 1786, and had a son who bore his name, who spent his life in Wilton, and died here February 2, 1847, in his eighty fourth year; leaving two sons, one of whom, Rev. Stephen Hubbell, was then nearly seventeen years in the Ministry. The older son, Wakeman, was yet to be Deacon. Deacon Hubbell was evidently an active, reliable, influential man. But tradition has preserved little of his services. The house in which he, his children and theirs, lived in Pimpewaug, for above a hundred years, has just been sold.

Some yet living remember Dea. *Daniel Gregory*, who was chosen Deacon, Oct. 7, 1794, and at once inducted into office. His relation to Dea. Matthew Gregory has already been mentioned. He was the grandfather of William D. Gregory. In the place of an older one, he built the house on the hill west of this house of worship, in which the latter lives.* He died April 18, 1821, at the age of seventy-eight. He united with the Church August 5, 1764, so that he was a member fifty-seven years, and a Deacon twenty-seven. His wife, Esther

---

* His children were Abigail, Elijah, Giles, Clark, Daniel and Sherman.

Hickok, supposed to be the granddaughter of Dea. Benjamin
Hickok, was a fitting helper in every good work, and died
May 13, 1822, at the age of seventy-seven years. Deacon
Gregory believed in covenant mercies, and a granddaughter
gratefully remembered many years after, his frequent prayer
for his "children and his children's children unto the third and
fourth generation." He was a thrifty farmer, given to hospitality.

Dea. *Jesse St. John* was a soldier of the Revolution, and a
member of one of the two "forlorn hopes" of twenty men
each, which volunteered to lead the attack in that desperate
but brilliant surprise and capture of Stony Point, on the
night of July 16th, 1779, by General Anthony Wayne.
Deacon St. John was not tall, but strongly built, capable of
enduring much fatigue; a man of few words and resolute in
purpose. As late as 1841 he would walk from his home,
west of the lower part of Belden's Hill, two and a half miles,
to attend a Preparatory lecture in a hot day in summer.
Soon after that time he removed to Brooklyn, E. D. (N. Y.),
to spend the remainder of his life with his son Thomas St.
John. His death occurred about 1846. His wife was Anna
Weed, to whom he was married Sept. 28, 1790. She died
the 18th of March, 1829, aged 73 years.

Dea. *John Chapman* was born in that part of Fairfield
which is now in Westport, in March, 1759. He married
Susannah Fitch, daughter of James Fitch of Norwalk, and
about 1790 removed to Chestnut Hill, where he lived in the
house now occupied by his son-in-law, Mr. Asahel Dudley, till
his death, April 13th, 1816. Mrs. Chapman was born Dec.
24th, 1756, and died March 14, 1833. They had four children, Anna H. (Mrs. Dudley), James Fitch, John and Clark M.
, One who knew him well says: "Deacon Chapman was erect, six
feet two inches in height, muscular and broad shouldered, of
commanding presence, calm, even tempered but very resolute,
energetic and industrious. Decided in his opinions, he was
yet gentle in his family, who loved and venerated him. An
excellent singer, he was regularly in his place in the choir on

Sunday. After a hard day's work he would go to Norwalk on business, and on his way home, forgetful of time, spend several hours at the house of some friend in singing. Fond of home, of a retiring disposition, he seldom took the lead unless evidently called by duty. His Christian character was marked and consistent."

His son, John Chapman, inherited his father's love for music, and led the choir fifty years ago. Both he and James F. were much respected. They went into business in New York, and died there; the latter, at the age of 55 years, Sept. 29, 1847. Tradition says the house in which Deacon Chapman lived was built about 1745. It was used early in the Revolution as a storehouse for some Norwalk goods. At the time of the burning of Danbury, a scouting party entered it and destroyed many of the goods.

Dea. *Matthew Marvin*, the sixth in descent from that Matthew Marvin who, coming to this country in 1635,* in the ship *Increase*, Robert Lea, master, settled at Hartford; the fifth in descent from that Matthew Marvin who, at the age of eight years, came with his father from England, and, at the age of twenty-four, came one of the first settlers to Norwalk; was the son of that Matthew Marvin who, about 1760, came from Norwalk and built the house in Pimpewaug, in which the son Matthew was born and died, and in which Dea. Charles Marvin now lives. He fitted for College with his Pastor (Mr. Lewis), graduated at Yale in 1785, went into business at Hudson, N. Y., returned to Wilton at the death of his father (1791), and for twenty-five years engaged with remarkable success in mercantile affairs, and for the remainder of his life was active in public and especially in Church and Society matters; the honored citizen, the trusted counsellor, the faithful deacon till his death, which occurred in the eighty-second year of his age,† on the 5th of June, 1842; less than a month after the great ingathering following the revival of that year, into which he had entered with the activity of a younger man. Deacon Marvin or "Esquire

---

* Dr. N. Bouton's Hist. Disc. at Norwalk, 1851, p. 71.
† He was baptized January 11th, 1761.

Marvin," as he was more frequently called, was tall, well proportioned, dignified and courteous in manner, active, clear-headed and resolute; by natural gifts, by education, and by possession of property well fitted to exercise an extraordinary and salutary influence in the parish and town.

Dea. *Zadok Raymond*, son of Clapp Raymond, born about 1764, united with the Church in 1811, and lived in Kent, in the house now for many years occupied by Charles Comstock; but in his later life in the first house on the road leading to Hurlbutt street, formerly occupied by his brother, Asahel Raymond, where he died April 12th, 1841, at the age of seventy-seven. He was a man, humble, devout and beloved, much interested in benevolent work. The Pastor of this Church may remember when, on a bright Summer's morning in 1832, two boys, who went on an errand to Deacon Raymond's, waited without, until he had ended worship in the family and with the men who had come to work in the hay-field. He evidently believed that the hired laborer might enjoy and be benefited by such service. He loved good men, and his house was often open for Sunday five o'clock and other neighborhood prayer-meetings.

Dea. *Jonathan Middlebrook* was the son of Michael Middle-brook, who came to Wilton from Fairfield, and, by the Half-Way Covenant, united with the Church June 1st, 1766. Jonathan Middlebrook united with the Church during the ministry of Mr. Woodward. The date of his election to the office of Deacon is not found.

His liberal gift to the fund of the Society has already been noticed. He gave also the land for the burying yard on the hill. He was by occupation a farmer. He died (without children) January 20th, 1832, at the age of seventy-seven years. His residence was on the Ridgefield road, east side, next to the Davenport place.

Dea. *Lewis H. St. John* united with this Church in 1816, was chosen Deacon in 1841, and ordained the 17th of October of that year.

He was a quiet, earnest, spiritually minded man, a little

above the average height, with a soft, pleasant voice, and gained the respect and good will of the people. His residence was in Nod. He was by trade a cooper, and tilled the land.

Deacon St. John died August 10th, 1867, aged seventy-four years.

Dea. *James Betts* was born in Wilton. His father, David Betts, died while he was yet a boy. By great energy and self-denial he secured an education at the Academy, attended lectures in New Haven, and early began to teach. Some time after Mr. Hawley Olmstead had removed to New Haven, Mr. Betts rented his former residence, and brought to it his Family School for Boys. In 1844 he built a commodious house in Stamford, where he yet remains. His school has been remarkably prosperous. One son, William J., graduated at Yale, 1870, and another, Alsop Lockwood, a member of the Class of 1872, died in College. Deacon Betts was received to the Church in 1825, was elected and ordained Deacon in 1841. In Stamford for thirty-two years he has well represented this Church and its influence upon its children.

Dea. *Giles Gregory* was born the 7th of October, 1806, and died February 20th, 1859. He was the youngest son of Moses and Abigail Gregory, the great-grandson (on his father's side) of Dea. Matthew Gregory; on his mother's side, the grandson of Dea. Daniel Gregory. He was thus descended by each parent from one of the elder Deacons—Dea. Matthew Gregory and Dea. Benjamin Hickok. He was educated at the Academy, taught school many years, and, after his father's death in 1837, engaged actively as a farmer. He confessed Christ, May, 1842, was ordained Deacon the 2d of November, 1849, and was active in Church, Society, and town affairs. His readiness to render pecuniary or personal aid to the poor, or those in distress, was hearty and efficient. His prayers indicated unfeigned humility; his life testified to the genuineness of his faith. His early death, which occurred February 19th, 1859, from typhoid fever, was lamented by many. He resided with his sisters in the house built by, or for his grandfather, Ezra Gregory, about 1740, but was never married.

Dea. *Wakeman Hubbell*, the son of Nathan and Sarah Hubbell, was born in Wilton. He was firm, conscientious and earnest to a high degree. He was elected to the office of Deacon on the 8th of February, 1860, and ordained the 19th of March following, by his old Pastor, Rev. Sylvanus Haight. Of his character and work I will speak in another connection.

Of those now in office—

Dea. Charles Marvin, who was ordained Oct. 17, 1841;

Dea. Benajah Gilbert, ordained March 19, 1860;

Dea. Edward Olmstead, ordained May 1, 1870; and

Dea. Robert T. B. Easton, ordained May 1, 1870,

you will not expect me to speak. Of the first three, whom I have long been permitted to regard as personal friends, it were easier for me to speak than to refrain. I may only say of the four, "their works praise them," and their Pastor is to be congratulated in having such counsellors and assistants in his work.

Indeed, it may be said, the Deacons of this Church have (so far as I am informed) rarely, if ever, been wanting in fidelity to the Pastor or to the Church, or given occasion to the reproach that has of late years, justly or unjustly, in some parts of the country, fallen upon this ancient and most important office, instituted by the Apostles of our Lord. One reason of their excellence may have been that the brethren here have so generally regarded the office as high and holy, which they shrunk from undertaking.

Before 1816 there was not in Wilton what was distinctly known as a Sabbath-school. About that time the influence of revivals, which organized the Missionary Society of Connecticut in 1798, the American Board in 1810, the American Bible Society, and what is now the Connecticut Home Missionary Society in 1816, began to organize schools for instruction, on the Lord's day, of the children of the poor and irreligious parents, who commonly neglected public worship. In most parishes this work was unfortunately not undertaken by the Church as such, but by individuals, usually Church-members acting with the consent and ·by the advice of the Pastor, and soon or late forming some association or organization to do this work, without any direct regard to the Church, to which the whole business properly belonged.

Sixty years ago such a beginning was made here. We may be sure that Mr. Haight led, and that some of the excellent women * were engaged in it. Garments and shoes were prepared. When all was ready on Sunday morning a number of children from Huckleberry Hills and elsewhere flocked to the house of Mr. Nathan Davenport to put them on, and go in order to Sunday-school. At the close of public worship, they returned to the house, exchanged their new garments for their old ones, and went home, to think of what they had seen and heard, and repeat the process next Sabbath. This, of course, could last only a little while. But the school thus begun has grown strong and useful to this day. Comparatively few have entered the Church in thirty years, who had not been members of the Sunday-school A list of its officers, teachers and pupils from the beginning, would contain the names of many whom we love to hold in lasting honor. And it will not, I trust, seem invidious; if, singling out from the list one who, more than forty years as teacher or superintendent, was almost always at his post, till death suddenly carried him away in 1869, I mention the name of *Wakeman Hubbell.*† Loyalty to truth, as he saw the truth, and to duty were conspicuous in his character. On a moderate amount of evidence it were easy to believe, that he consciously or unconsciously allowed himself to be influenced by those memorable words, which should have been cut into the grave-stone of that Mr. John St. John, the father of Bela St. John, who perhaps eighty years ago, when rallied by one of the ma-

---

* Miss Susan Comstock, daughter of Strong Comstock, and Miss Dolly Gregory, daughter of Moses Gregory, were, it is believed, active in this enterprise. Some years later Miss Comstock went, under the care of the American Board to the "Great Osage Mission," which was in Missouri and Arkansas. In October, 1822, she married Mr. (afterwards Rev) William C. Reqna, who was then Assistant Missionary. ~he was for some time in the service, and died, if I remember, at Little Rock, Arkansas. Miss Gregory desired to go with Miss Comstock, and attended the Company as far as New Jersey. She was in Wilton, in the day-school and Sunday-school, an efficient teacher till failing health and other causes prevented longer service.

† He died suddenly in the field, Nov. 2, 1869, in the 71st year of his age.

jority for having voted, by rising, alone against the others, in a meeting of the Society, promptly replied : " If I am wrong, I ought to be alone ; but if I am right, I am not ashamed to be alone."

It would be appropriate to this occasion, if time allowed, to mention the names of those who, by birth or adoption, belong to Wilton, who graduated at some college or literary institution or professional school, or who studied law, medicine or theology, or became authors, or were married to one of that class. . I have prepared a table containing their names. Some of them were never members of this congregation, but they belonged to families once included in this parish, or were themselves for a longer or shorter period members of the Wilton Academy. Additions to that table will be welcome.

But among the many who were born and nurtured under the shadow of this Church, though not himself a member, whose subsequent life shed distinguished honor upon this town, none is more conspicuous than MOSES STUART; whom it would ill befit us to pass without notice to-day. He was born in 1780, in the house now owned and occupied by Abijah M. Jones, the son of Isaac and Olive Stuart. He read books with eagerness when four years old, but remained a farmer's boy with no thought of college, till, at fourteen, a thirst for knowledge was manifest which neither toil or years could quench. He went to Norwalk,* made rapid progress in the rudiments of Latin and French, and was fitted for the Sophomore class by Roger Minot Sherman, who had the preceding year been a tutor at Yale. He graduated with the highest honor in the class of 1799, afterwards he taught in what was North Fairfield, and in Danbury ; studied law, was admitted to the bar at Danbury in 1802 ; became tutor at Yale from 1802 to 1804. There and afterwards he showed almost unsurpassed skill in awakening the enthusiasm of young men in their studies. But here the Spirit of the Lord met him and he heard the call which Paul heard—to preach

---

* Prof. Park's sermon at his funeral

the Gospel. He united with the College Church and studied theology with Dr. Dwight. His first and only settlement was as Pastor of the First Church in New Haven. It was an era (those almost four years of his pastorate are yet remembered there), during which above one hundred and seventy (172) were added to the Church by profession. His successor, Rev. Dr. N. W. Taylor, forty years later, spoke in the highest terms of his power as a preacher, reckoning him second to none in this country. In 1810 he was wanted, as Professor of Hebrew and Greek, in the new Theological Seminary at Andover, Mass. "We cannot spare him," said one of the Yale Faculty to the Rev. Dr. Samuel Spring, of Newburyport, who had come to New Haven to get Mr. Stuart's assent to the plan. "We want no man who can be spared" was Dr. Spring's reply.

He went to Andover, as he himself said, with small knowledge of Hebrew, and of Greek Grammar less than many a student who this year enters college. In two years he had prepared a Hebrew Grammar, and, as there was no printer who understood the business, he was obliged to set a part of the types with his own hands.

The work that Mr. Stuart did for the Ministry and the Church in America, by promoting the study of the Bible in the original languages, and in awakening the enthusiasm of young men who were to be ministers, in the study of biblical philology, is one of the extraordinary things of this wonderful century. He studied German when his brethren in the ministry trembled lest he should be poisoned with German rationalism. They little dreamed that he was preparing thereby to set up an immovable barrier against Unitarianism, and other religious errors. The multiplicity and value of his labors during the almost forty-two years of his residence at Andover, till his death, after a brief illness, Jan. 4th, 1852, may be inferred from the discourse delivered at his funeral by Professor Edwards A. Park. A copy of it might well be in this Sunday-school Library, and in every family, that can appreciate the honor such a man confers upon his native town. Some may remember his occasionally preaching here many years ago. But the spirit of the man is seen in the words with which he closed " Two Sermons on the Atonement :" " When I behold the glory of the Saviour as revealed in the gospel, I am constrained to cry out with the believing Apostle, 'My Lord and My God !' And when my departing spirit shall quit these mortal scenes and wing its way to the world unknown, with my latest breath I desire to pray as the expiring martyr did, ' Lord Jesus, receive my spirit.' " [See also Prof. Phelps in the *Advance*, May, '76.]

There was, perhaps, fifty years ago, a society of ladies in which were active Mrs. Haight and Mrs. Matthew Marvin, to aid the American Education Society, of which I have not seen the record. By the influence of Mrs. Merwin, the Ladies Sewing Society, called the " Ladies Home Missionary Association," held its first meeting at the house of Mr. Wakeman Hubbell, Sept. 14th, 1836. Twenty ladies were present.* Mrs. Merwin was the first President, and Miss Clara M. Gregory, Secretary and Treasurer, which office she holds now ; † Mrs. Willard was President eighteen years, till her death ; Mrs. Wakeman Hubbell was President till called to her reward ; Mrs. Merwin is now President.

As a bond of sympathy among the sisters and families of the Church ; as an educator of the daughters who here or elsewhere have been called to labor for the Kingdom of Heaven ; as a means of raising funds for Home Missions and for other benevolent objects, and as an auxiliary in refitting this House of Worship ‡ in 1844 ; in building the Chapel, and in providing furniture for the two houses, the Ladies Society has been invaluable. It is worthy of mention that since 1856 the Society has raised above two thousand dollars. A list of its officers and the roll of its members would recall faces, and persons, by whose self-sacrificing labors and wise plans we are benefited to-day ; who (many here may say) bound our young hearts to them by cords stronger than death ; who should be praised, if the world has been the better for our

---

* See note.

† Mrs. Helen Comstock was for several years in that office.

‡ See Appendix.

living; whose names are now graven on the stones in the burying-ground; but whose best monuments are in the character and lives of the men and women of this assembly. Though "lost to sight," their presence is with us—a shield from temptation, an inspiration for duty.

But the time forbids me longer to trespass upon your attention; lest, like the "ancient mariner" of Coleridge, I cheat the hearers of the promised feast, which they may well be in haste to reach.

The Church, which our fathers planted here with fasting and prayer, one hundred and fifty years ago, has, by the good Providence of Him whose help they sought, not betrayed their trust, nor prematurely fallen into the decrepitude of an old age of poverty. It has borne precious fruit; it is still vigorous with youth. Its blossoms, that are the fullest of promise, may sometimes wither, and its ripe fruit be gathered by the heavenly gardener; but it is a tree drawing nourishment from the river of life. It has been highly favored with Pastors who were sound in the Faith—men of education, whom the Master had endowed for their work; and who, with a single unhappy exception, continued faithful unto death. It has steadfastly maintained the doctrines of the Gospel. In matters of religion, of education, in its testimony for temperance and for morality, its influence has blessed the town, in which for three-quarters of a century it was the only Church.

It has, since 1826, furnished at least eight men (six graduates of Yale, one of Williams, and one of Trinity) who are yet in the Ministry. Whatever sins may have been justly laid at the door of individual members, the records show, and tradition does not question that the Church, as a whole, has in the main been preserved from scandalous immoralities. It has not ceased to testify for Jesus, and to invite the weary and heavy-laden to share in the blessings of the Gospel. It has cheered the toils and wiped the tears of the living; it has strengthened the faith of the dying. The fathers and mothers have fallen asleep, and the children have risen in their place till five generations have come and gone from the house of the Lord. And yet this Church witnesses, that the promise is to us and our children ; and that, if they forsake not the God of their fathers, He will increase them more and more. Upon this fair heritage of hill and vale, refreshed by streams of water, and glorified by Christian homes, His face will continue to shine. The sons and daughters, who remain to worship on this hill of Zion, and to be buried amid their fathers' graves, and those whose lot is cast in other parts of the vineyard, will become precious stones and polished pillars in the spiritual temple, which forever ascendeth to the praise of God our Saviour, JESUS CHRIST.

The "Pilgrim Fathers" was then sung by Mr. ROBERT J. JOHNSTON.

The CHAIRMAN—*Ladies and Gentlemen:* Wilton, as you have heard, has been quite fruitful in Ministers. The Committee have selected one of them, who is of good Puritan descent, and bearing a good Puritan name, as the Poet of this occasion ; and I now present him to you—the Rev. JOHN G. DAVENPORT, of Bridgeport.

POEM.

WHO'D think, to see her beaming
 In her fresh and bright array,
That the Blessed Mother of us all
 Is a hundred and fifty to-day?

I've studied her somewhat closely,
 With loving and reverent care ;
But I've failed to discover a wrinkle
 Deforming her features so fair !

We're weaving a chaplet of honor,
 And crowning her with it now—
But it covers no thread of silver
 On her peaceful, radiant brow !

The stranger who'd not heard recounted
  The years and the changes she's seen,
Instead of a hundred and fifty
  Would think her but "sweet sixteen"!

How graciously she receives us!
  How warm is her welcome to-day!
We're ready to blush as we greet her,
  To think that—we went away!

But there's merit in separation—
  It's well for some children to roam;
No doubt she loves some of us better
  Than if we'd continued at home!

While so fresh and so youthful appearing,
  Her grasp neither feeble nor cold,
We're proud of our dignified mother
  In part from the fact that she's old!

Why, think of it! great is the honor,
  This famous Centennial time,
Of owning a table rheumatic
  Or a chair truly worth not a dime;

If only the ricketty pieces
  Have come from the years far away;
The sunlight of decades departed
  With gold plates them over to-day!

A tea-cup some General's moustache
  Brushed lightly a century ago,
Or a dress Mrs. Washington looked at,
  But didn't quite fancy, you know;

Or a snuff-box that, daintily handled,
  Beguiled the fair ladies of yore—
These things are esteemed above rubies
  In setting of costliest ore!

This year an old hat's in the fashion,
  Old houses are stylish and grand,
And I fear that old hearts, and not new ones,
  Are the prevalent mode of the land!

Reversed is the sentiment uttered
  To Paul's dear Corinthian fold,
New things have now passed away wholly,
  Lo, all things have now become *old!*

Since such *is* the public condition,
  And age is more precious than gold,
We're proud that our sacred Church mother
  Is a hundred and fifty years old!

They talk of the age of the Nation,
  And nudge all the world to recall
That it rounds out a century's existence
  Some time between now and next Fall!

But over their pomp and their bluster
  We Wiltoners slyly must laugh,
For, while they are keeping Centennial,
  We're keeping *Centennial and a half!*

As of "seventy-six" they are boasting,
  And telling its fame evermore,
We'd like to inquire the condition
  Of things half a century before!

Where then was the parchment conferring
  Independence on good "Uncle Sam"?
Why, the sheep that afterward wore it
  As yet wasn't even a lamb!

Where then was the pen bravely wielded
  For Freedom, oppressed and forlorn?
The goose from whose pinions it fluttered
  Was still with the millions unborn!

And the hands that subscribed to the Charter,
  Equal liberty claiming for all,
As yet had not managed a top-string
  Nor directed the flight of a ball!

And where was the bell, at whose fracture
  The nations now reverently stare?
Not yet were its particles blended
  The pounding and pealing to share!

The tree that, though hacked with the hatchet,
  Will live while the ages shall die,
Was a cherry-stone then, just rejected
  From good Mother Washington's pie!

Ben Franklin, whose wisdom to honor
  The world now indulges the right,
Was *still wearing* the garments that furnished
  The tail of his thunderstruck kite!

The illustrious army of heroes
  That battled so bravely and well,
As infantry yet were unmarshalled
  On the day of whose honors we tell!

Not one of the stars of our banner
  Had yet risen over the land,
Not a stripe of the snow or the crimson
  Our Nation's horizon had spanned!

Enwrapped in the mists of the future,
  Its grandeur and beauty concealed,
Our Royal Republic was waiting
  Till Time should a coronet yield!

This Church, at its birth, was a subject
  Of England's imperial sway;
To the First of the Georges it hastened,
  Its loyal obedience to pay!

Just think of it! four of its Pastors
  Were wont to the altar to bring
The earnest petition, "God bless him,
  Our Sovereign Master the King!"

And the fourth may have finally added,
  "Please bless him—he needs it, we know—
But help us to strike the old tyrant
  A blinding and withering blow!"

Thus the brow of our mother was touched
  With the kiss of the long ago,
And on her to-day our reverent love
  We eagerly all bestow.

O, child of the far-off years!
  O, mother benign and true!
With tender and grateful hearts
  Acknowledging all thy due;

Acknowledging all we owe
  To thy long and faithful years,
To the truth thou hast patiently maintained,
  Though it cost thee pain and tears,

Not in our name alone,
  But of all whom thou hast blessed,
Thy family scattered far to-day,
  We hail thee "worthiest," "best!"

Our gratulations we bring thee
  With regard that can never be told—
God bless thee to-day, good mother,
  A hundred and fifty years old!

The Historian here has told us
  (Though we scarce can think it, still)
That our good Church hasn't always dwelt
  On this consecrated hill!

For many a year her mansion
  Was a mile or two farther down,
But at length she thought it needful
  To see to this part of the town!

Thus often I've noticed a mother
  Removing her easy chair
From a group of orderly children
  Toward certain demanding her care!

Just how it may be at the present
  I haven't the power to explain,
But perhaps if she followed "the leadings"
  She'd quickly return again!

My childhood was very familiar
  With the scene of her primal abode,
Though scarce a tradition suggested
  The place where her altars had glowed.

No doubt as a bare-footed urchin,
  In perfect *abandon* of play,
I often have trampled "regardless"
  The spot where her "corner-stone" lay.

No doubt I have often been merry
  (Such thoughts strange emotions infuse)
Just where the good Parson, my grandsire,
  As a "candidate" shook in his shoes!

And there in the shady pasture,
  Where his words, like dew distilled,
Not thinking of spiritual sustenance,
  My basket with berries I filled!

I wonder that, in the stillness
  Of the Summer afternoon,
I caught no echo of the past—
  No snatch of pious tune!

That 'mid the ferns, and through the hedge,
   And o'er the ledges bare,
There breathed no word of holy truth—
   No pleading voice of prayer !

'Twould seem that sun- and star-light
   Must there forever rise,
Like shimmering golden ladder rounds
   'Twixt earth and Paradise !

For sacred evermore must be
   The spot where Saints prepare,
With sigh and psalm and sacrament
   Heaven's ministries to share !

Where stood the second house of prayer—
   Just off the broad highway—
My childish feet have often roved
   At hour of setting day !

For where the Pastor fed his flock,
   And warned from snares and sloughs,
There, through the purple twilight shade,
   I homeward drove the cows !

And oft I seemed to hear again
   The words that thrilled of yore—
The testimony holy men
   To Christ's redemption bore !

And oft beside the Pastor's grave
   I knelt to read his fame,
And wished his virtues might descend
   On all who bear his name !

And as I saw him in the midst,
   His *Church asleep* around,
I wondered if 'twere ever thus
   Within their temple found !

The spot is hallowed evermore,
   Where flock and shepherd lie,
And silent wait till fadeless dawn
   Illume the Eastern sky.

O you who hold the ancient trust,
   Who still the homestead keep,
I pray you, guard with pious care
   Th' enclosure where they sleep!

Nor let the flaunting sumach there
   Display its crimson shield,
Nor to the tramp of feeding brute
   The precious acre yield!

There slumber staid and saintly sires,
   There dames of gentler grace;
They ask (what less can we bestow?)
   An honored resting-place.

Wherever else our mother dwelt,
   This, this to us is home,
And dearer far than minster grand
   Of stateliest tower and dome!

Converges here the Sabbath light
   Of years long flown away,
Illuming the familiar scene
   With sweetest, holiest ray!

Bright verdure now, and fragrant flowers,
   Our holy altars twine;
But mem'ry decks, with fadeless bloom,
   The consecrated shrine!

These sacred aisles, with reverent step,
   Our infant feet have trod;
We deemed them, as they were, the paths
   That lead to heaven and God.

These pews—I weary now to think
   How much of them I bore,
With head upon the rail, and feet
   Some inches from the floor!

Good Parson Smith a marvel seemed,
   He had so much to say!
Relief I sought in fennel-seed
   And blessed caraway!

But sanctuary oak grew soft
   As, following good advice,
I to the *Pastor's sermon* turned
   For my supply of spice.

I this believe, I say it for
   The good of restless youth,
The softest cushion for a pew,
   Is a wish to hear the truth!

At noon, along these galleries
   In Sunday-school we met,
The girls and boys on either side
   In opposition set!

They thought it wise, perhaps it was,
   The pupils so to place—
That with a gulf between, they looked
   .Each other in the face!

But possibly occasion rose,
   For some to humbly pray
Amid their lessons "Turn mine eyes
   From seeing vanity!"

If I am right, 'twas brother Mix,
   To his cognomen true,
Who brought us to the floor below
   And rearranged us too!

But I shall never once forget
　　The day I joined the school,
And gave my name to be enrolled
　　According to the rule!

" What's man's chief end? " the teacher asked;
　　'Twas more than I could meet;
I hung my head and steadfast gazed
　　Upon my swinging feet!

Perhaps he thought in pantomime
　　I thus essayed reply;
' Twas not my toes—and to the next
　　He turned with heavy sigh!

Though I was stupid, he was good,
　　And his successors all,
The truths they taught shall light my path
　　When death-shades 'round me fall!

When first I sought the House of God
　　The choir seemed rather gay,
The fiddle and the viol were there
　　With Dr. Mead to play!

Perhaps I am not orthodox,
　　But I could never see
Why we to Satan's use should yield
　　Their stirring melody!

The Psalmist used an " instrument "
　　" With strings" that numbered " ten "!
What reason is there, one with four
　　Should be forbidden then?

I well remember when the first
　　Melodeon arrived,
How strange it seemed that until then
　　Without it we'd survived!

But soon one more pretentious came,
   Our Arthur * was its king,
His magic fingers swept the keys
   And made the rafters ring!

But what now fills its honored place
   And moves the ear to bliss?
I see no *Tribune* statement here
   That " not an Organ—this."

I thought that Darwin's great idea
   Was scarcely proven true,
But surely here's a striking case
   That bids us think anew!

Consider the " development"
   Within so brief a while,
Of this Grand Johnston Organ †
   From Dr. Mead's bass-viol!

O Organ! wilderness of tubes,
   With all thy glorious sweep
Thy myriad loftier harmonies
   Thy pealing thunders deep!

Swell thou His praise who lives and reigns
   Though generations die!
Our lagging hallelujahs lift
   E'en to His courts on high!

Exulting greet the Sabbath morn
   Oft as it dawns again!
Console the mourner with thy sobs,
   Speed the glad bridal train!

Reflect the sorrow and the joy
   Our loved ones here shall feel,

---

* Dr. Arthur Barrows of New York.

† Mr. Johnston, the Chorister, took the initiative in procuring an Organ in which he was heartily supported. It was built by Geo. W. Earle, Riverhead, L. I.

Inspire to high and sacred art,
    To patriotic zeal!

Thus breathe a blessing from thy tubes
    On all who gather here,
Till heaven's eternal harmonies
    Break on their ravished ear!

What sacred and tender memories throng
    This consecrated space! *
Cherubic and glorious wings must e'er
    O'ershadow the holy place!

Here has the smiling and dimpled babe
    To Him been lovingly given,
Who said "Permit the children to come
    For of such is the highest heaven."

Here scores and hundreds have boldly stood,
    To acknowledge their Master's name,
And solemnly consecrate themselves
    To the spread of His peerless fame!

And here has the chosen Pastor bowed
    His neck to the yoke of care!
The burden great of his people's weal
    Thenceforward to meekly bear!

And here has the blushing maiden said
    To him who would have it so,
" To leave thee again entreat me not—
    For whither thou goest, I'll go!"

And here with a gaze unspeakably sad
    And blinded with bitter tears
We have looked our last at the peaceful face
    That had brightened our life for years.

---

* Between the pulpit and the pews.

O, many a sacred and holy spot
　　This beautiful earth·can boast,
But to scores here met—this Altar of God
　　Is the place that is hallowed most!

Our brother has summoned to view
　　The men who have ministered here,
And their names as he called them, one by one,
　　Fell musically on the ear!

And their forms as they slowly passed
　　By his magic word invoked!
Seemed loftier than the sons of men
　　And in saintlier purity cloaked.

A lingering lustre clings
　　To the spot where they plead for truth,
And sought for the Master—manhood's strength
　　And the fiery heart of youth!

A mantle of glory descends
　　On the Pastor.that ministers here,
Whose folds so radiant e'er have wrapped
　　The worthy and the dear!

No surplice of shimmering white
　　Nor robe that a prelate wore,
Compares with this tribute of love and power
　　From those who have gone before!

Forgive me, but I recall
　　A day when this mantle of might,
Less warmly *I* here desired, than one
　　That should bury me out of sight!

For on this very desk
　　As an altar of sacrifice,
My first-born sermon I offered up
　　With countless fears and sighs!

Paul spoke of the "feeble knees"—;
   And I well knew what he meant,
For mine beneath their weight of woe
   Like reeds in a tempest bent !

And David tells of the tongue
   That cleaves to the roof of the mouth,
And mine seemed firmly packed
   In the dust of an August drouth !

" You'll find my text," said I,
   And thereupon all grew dim,
And I scarce could tell if 'twas Holy Writ
   That I needed to give, or a hymn !

And the congregation danced
   And whirled in a curious way,
Decidedly festive it seemed to me
   For the holy Sabbath day !

And I thought—an earthquake now,
   If such a thing could be—
Would bring a fitting reward to them
   And a great relief to me !

My heart—it quaked instead !
   And I labored my sermon through,
And it seemed that ere I could say " Amen"
   The sunset would be due !

But the agony closed at last,
   And I found as I went away,
That while I claimed to have suffered,
   The people thought it was they !

And so this sacred desk
   O'er which bright memories break
I still must regard, somewhat,
   As the martyr regards the stake !

Thus coming hither to-day
 We hasten the mansion round,
And every part of the dear old home
 O'erflowing with interest is found!

I scarcely doubt that some—
 E'en paused in the vestibule,
And thought "Just here she took my arm
 At the close of the singing-school!"

And others reflected thus—
 "Can it be that it was so?
That on this spot she turned away
 With a sharply answered 'No'?"

How much of the joy and the sorrow
 The doubt and the hope and the fear,
That our lives have known in the time gone by
 Must centre forever here!

To-day we look, how vainly,
 For faces once beaming here;
We close our eyes and they come again,
 With their olden smile, draw near.

Fathers and mothers, sweet and grave—
 Who loved the House of God—
Dear youths that early sought their rest
 Beneath the daisied sod!

The men who bore along these aisles
 The consecrated bread!
The trusting shepherd who, his flock,
 To peaceful pastures led!

The little child with pattering feet—
 The strong man in his pride,
The school-boy with his modest air,
 The blissful, blooming bride!

They come again! we see them take
 The place they filled of old,
A large and precious portion
 Of this dear flock and fold!

We look again! It was a dream!
 Their faces melt in air!
But hark! a voice celestial breathes
 " Look up! they're gathered there!"

O, brothers, sisters, blest the tie,
 That binds us to our home;
That to this household links us still
 Where'er our feet may roam!

And blest the immortal tie that binds
 To that dear shadowy throng,
That, just a little farther on
 In life, has passed along!

These silken chords our hearts will draw
 Toward all that's good and true,
Till we with those we love shall meet
 Beyond the arch of blue!

And so, dear Mother Church,
 We cluster round thy knee;
And pray thee bless us every one
 Thy loyal family.

Our filial love for thee
 Is pure as the purest gold,
God bless thee our precious mother,
 A hundred and fifty years old!

The exercises of the morning were concluded with singing
"Old Hundred."

EXERCISES AFTER COLLATION.

The CHAIRMAN—The Committee having bestowed upon me full autocratic power, and all here feeling, I suppose, pretty comfortable after the bountiful collation which has been furnished by the ladies, I shall undertake to call upon some of you to give us a little after-dinner talk—nothing eloquent, but good, plain, humorous, pleasant after-dinner talk.

Now, the next best thing to being born and living here, I think, is to marry a wife in Wilton; and I see in the audience a gentleman who had that rare good fortune. Rev. Mr. MIX will please come forward.

The reverend gentleman acknowledged his position in fitting words, extending affectionate greetings from the Presbyterian Church in Orange, N. J., of which he is Pastor.

The CHAIRMAN—*Ladies and Gentlemen:* I want to say a word about Ministers. When I was a boy, and they used to stand up in the pulpit, pretty high up, with plenty long sermons, I don't know why, but somehow or other I didn't get a very good impression of them; but since, as I have walked through life with them on the same plane, I find that there is in the Ministers of to-day a good deal of human nature, and I don't know as they are very much worse than the generality of men. I have a love and respect for the old school of Ministers, and we fortunately have one of them with us here to-day—a gentleman who commenced the academical course of his education, as I understand, at the Wilton Academy almost at its foundation, and who has taken high rank in the profession to which he has devoted the energies of a long and well-spent life. I present to you the Rev. Dr. BOUTON, of Concord, New Hampshire.

REMARKS OF REV. DR. BOUTON.

Mr. PRESIDENT: I wish, first of all, to thank the Committee and the good people of Wilton for giving me an invitation to attend this Anniversary. Within five minutes after I received your invitation I said, "I will go," and I repeated it to my family as soon as I met them, "I am going to Wilton." Well, a little wonder was expressed why I should be so interested to go to Wilton, but I told them that I had an interest in Wilton, and an interest that would lead me there on this occasion. I have a long time, Mr. President and people of Wilton, I have a long time carried a burden which has weighed upon me whenever I have thought of it. I am greatly in debt to Wilton, and I have wished for an opportunity to pay that debt in such coin as is at my command. I will tell you what that debt is, if you will indulge me in a few moments' remarks. Perhaps it may take a little longer time than the gentleman took who *mixed* things up. But to begin, sir. I have an interest in Wilton on the ground of soil. I am accustomed to look somewhat at old records, and I looked at the old Connecticut records—the Colony records of Connecticut—and I found when in May, 1726, a petition was presented to the General Court of Connecticut for the laying off of the parish of Wilton from the town of Norwalk into a village (that was the language), the line ran through Richard Bouton's and Joseph (or some other name) Betts' land, and Richard Bouton's came within the bounds of this village of Wilton. Well, who was Richard Bouton? He was a son of the original ancestor of the Bouton name, settled in Norwalk, John Bouton, Senior. And besides that particular connection there was another on which I claim a still higher and deeper interest than even that, for Richard Bouton was the grandson of Matthew Marvin, Senior—himself of Norwalk, but whose descendants are here—and Matthew Marvin is an honored name in the town of Wilton, long to be remembered by this people. Well, now it just happened in this way. That John Bouton, Senior, came over the same year (1635) with Matthew Marvin. They went together to the town of Hartford, and there remained till 1651. Together John Bouton and Matthew Marvin were admitted as freemen in the Colony of Connecticut the same year and at the same session of the Court. They came to Norwalk together in 1651. In 1656 John Bouton married the daughter of Matthew Marvin, and Rich-

ard Bouton was the son of John, so that Matthew Marvin,
Senior, was the grandfather of Richard Bouton; and in that
line I stand, so that I claim a right of soil in Wilton and a
relationship to some of your best families.

Well, now, a little further, Mr. President. I said I owe a
great debt to Wilton, and that debt came of my education.
I commenced study in 1817, and, while attending school a
little while at Norwalk and a little while at New Canaan, I
received an invitation from the Rev. Sylvanus Haight, bringing to me a message from Hawley Olmstead, inviting me to
come to the school which he had then recently opened just
across the road here. There is where I closed my preparation for college, and from there went with the recom-
mendation of my honored instructor, Hawley Olmstead, and
was received into Yale College.

While I am speaking on that subject, I wish to say that
then my debt was contracted. I became acquainted with
very many families in Wilton, and they were kind enough
to entertain me, and I never think of it but with feelings of
deepest gratitude and obligation to the good people of Wilton:
and I have often thought with myself, if I ever have an
opportunity I will pay that people for their kindness to me.
I was not a school-master then, but I boarded around by particular invitation; and I have tried to recall the names of the
families that were pleased so kindly to entertain me. I may
omit some of them—very likely I shall—but I will endeavor
to pay my debt by naming the great kindness of Matthew
Marvin and his family to me during that year of my residence here; to Captain William Sellick, who, I believe, lived
on the brow of Belden's Hill. The next name that I have is
Mr. Nathan Hubbell and his wife, never to be forgotten; and
I often thank the Lord that out of that family, perhaps,
partly the reward of a cup of cold water, if nothing more,
one of the sons that went to the Academy with me has been
an honored Minister of the Gospel for years, and I suppose is
still living. And then that beloved elder brother, Dea.
Wakeman Hubbell, who, the last time I was here, took me
all over town and reminded me here and there of the places

where I had been; and the Lord has put two of his sons into the Ministry. Besides Mr. Nathan Hubbell, I remember Mr. Levi Scribner and his wife, now among the oldest people of Wilton. God bless them in their old age—ninety-four, I am told, Mr. Scribner has attained to, and ninety his wife. Well then, again, I remember the Middlebrooks (Jonathan I believe the name was) up on this road towards Ridgefield, and the Comstocks in another part of the town, and Mr. Lewis Betts in the western part of the town—all of whom entertained me, and I wish to thank them to-day, and out of the fulness of my heart I do thank them. I will tell you, Mr. President, that when I have been under the inspiration of the Ministry, and have felt like working for the Master, I have felt constantly the inspiration that came upon me—an inspiration of gratitude for the goo l people that helped me on in my education. And now I thank the people of Wilton, and all the descendants of those families and others, for their kindness to me in the days of my youth.

Well, among my memories, Mr. President, I remember certain excellent women of Wilton. I like all good women, always did, but there were some that were "*gooder*," at least I thought they were very good and I held them in very high esteem. Now, if the other ladies won't deem it invidious, I wish to name certain good women. I had a most profound respect and even reverence for the piety and good sense of Mrs. Matthew Marvin, and I held in equal honor, I think, Mrs. Nathan Hubbell, and I had a profound respect for the wife of the Rev. Sylvanus Haight. But among others I remember a Miss Dolly Gregory with great pleasure. I used to walk on the same road sometimes going to Mr. Sellick's and often fell in with Miss Dolly. There was this excellence about her; she was one of the active young women of this Church and she was one of the persons alluded to in the speech to-day, that took the liberty, perhaps with the consent of the Pastor, to open a Sunday-school. I had a Sunday-school off in this direction and she had one over in this direction. And then besides Miss Dolly Gregory there was Miss Dolly Hoyt and there was a Miss Susan Comstock.

They were remarkably pious and excellent young women, and those two last, having the grace of God in their hearts, the love of Christ burning in a flame there, were not content to minister to Sunday-schools in Wilton, but went out as missionaries, and I suppose, spent their lives and died as missionary teachers.

Well, now, there are certain other reminiscences of which I would speak. I wish to say that there was no man in my youth, no man in later years, for whom I entertained a higher respect and a higher reverence than for Hawley Olmstead, Esq. He esteemed me more highly than I deserved, but, I am sure, I loved him not more than he deserved. I heard the first prayer that he ever offered in his school, and it so impressed me at the time, that I remember to this day one sentence in it, and that was, I think, in these very words: "That we might consider ourselves as strangers and sojourners upon earth, a lodging place only for the night until the day dawn that shall never end." That was one petition in his prayer.

Well, then, of Rev. Sylvanus Haight, sir, he was my friend. He took me by the hand, he opened the way for me to go into that school, and Mr. Haight was my friend as long as he lived. I look upon it as one of the remarkable favors of Divine Providence, that I was permitted to be with him and to offer prayer with him just before he died. It came to pass in this way. I started on my way for the Christian Commission in 1864, and heard on the way that Mr. Haight was sick. I immediately went to his chamber. There he was lying upon his sick-bed, and as all supposed his dying-bed. I talked with him a few moments, expressed my thanks to him for his goodness to me, and then said he, "Will you pray?" I knelt down by his bedside, putting my hands upon the pillow where he was dying, and next morning the news came to me; Mr. Haight is dead. Well, now, about his eloquence, about his character as a preacher. I could heartily respond to what was said by the historian to-day in several respects, and I have an impression to this day of one of those sermons. It was on the Judgment Day. He rose in that sermon to a very high pitch of eloquence; it was solemnly and awfully impressive. I remember, on that occasion, speaking about the solemnity of the Great Day of Judgment, he said, among other things, "It seems to me that no man can look forward to the scenes of the Judgment without a degree of fear and trembling. I am sure I cannot." Well, there was Mrs. Elias Betts, one of the most remarkably pious women that I ever knew, and under that sermon, overwhelmed as she was, she literally went away trembling, and to her, above almost any Christian woman I ever knew, might be applied the language of the Prophet or the language of God through the Prophet, "The High and lofty One who inhabiteth eternity dwelleth in the high and holy Place, yet also with him that is of a contrite and humble spirit and that trembleth at my word." That Christian wo-man always trembled under God's great truth.

Well, Mr. President, I will not enlarge; I have taken up too much time already, but I desire to repeat again my thanks to the good people of Wilton for their kindness to me in the days of my youth, and for the inspiration that their aid gave me, to do what was in my power for the cause of the Blessed Master.

I ought to say that in that regard I have not been without a blessing. After completing my college course I went directly to Andover Theological Seminary and the very day that I closed my studies at Andover I received application from a gentleman to go as a candidate to the Church in Concord, New Hampshire. I went and have been there to this time. I was Pastor of the First Church forty-two years, and then resigned. In that period God blessed my labors so far that over seven hun-dred were admitted to the Church of which I was Pastor, a larger number were baptized, and I have had a very happy relation with that people, never a ripple on the surface of things from the day of my ordination till this time. Having resigned my pastorate after forty-two years, I am now one of the parish-ioners, sitting every Sabbath in my seat, and conscious, through the goodness of God, of having the favor still of the people, and though I resigned my situation after forty-two years of service, I have been well employed during the last ten years, and hope through the goodness of God to do a little more service for the Master. During all the time I have never been sick. I have never been laid aside from my work. I have been enabled to go in and out year after year without any interruption, and so having obtained help of the Lord I continue till this day. I may never have another opportunity, but this I say truly and heartily to this beloved people, I thank you for your goodness to me, and I bid the children and children's children of those who helped me farewell.

Two verses of "All hail the power of Jesus' name" was sung to *Coronation*, in which the congregation heartily joined.

The CHAIRMAN—This Church is so closely connected with the Norwalk Church, I believe a good many of you here would like to hear from some one from that town. I call on the Rev. Mr. DUNNING of South Norwalk.

In the absence of the Rev. Mr. Hamilton of the First Church, Norwalk, the Parent Church, Mr. DUNNING gracefully responded for the *South Norwalk* Church, the youngest of the five daughters.

The CHAIRMAN—The ministers and teachers and doctors have had something to say here, and now I think the lawyers ought to be heard. I understand Mr. EUGENE SMITH of New York is in the house, and he will now address you.

Mr. SMITH obeyed, and in well-chosen words confessed to the bonds which tie him to the spot of his boyhood years.

Mr. N. M. BELDEN of Southport, Dr. Bela ST. JOHN of Wolcottville, and C. L. WESTCOTT, Esq., of New York, answered to their names when called upon, and bore grateful testimony to the joy and glory of the occasion which had brought them here.

Rev. Mr. Willard then read a letter from Rev. Mr. HARVEY, also a list of Wiltonian graduates from different American colleges; after which the choir and congregation joined in singing "Hold the Fort," and the audience was dismissed with the benediction by Rev. Mr. MERWIN.

APPENDIX.

I.

The names of the signers of the petition, that Wilton might be constituted a "parish or village," were:

JOSEPH ELMER,	DANIEL TROWBRIDGE,
JOSEPH JUMP,	NATHAN OLMSTEAD,
DANIEL ABBOTT,	STEPHEN BUCKINGHAM,
JOSEPH CARLE,	JOHN STUART,
JOHN KEELER,	BENJAMIN HICKOK,
MATTHEW ST. JOHN,	RICHARD BOUTON,
DAVID KEELER,	OBADIAH WOOD,
JOHN ST. JOHN,	THOMAS BOUTON,
DAVID BETTS,	JAMES TROWBRIDGE,
SAMUEL BETTS, JR.,	JONATHAN STURDEVANT,
STEPHEN BETTS,	RALPH KEELER,
NATHANIEL SLAUSON,	JACHIN GREGORY,
JOHN WOOD, JR.,	JOHN DUNNING,
JONATHAN WOOD, JR.,	NATHANIEL KETCHUM,
NATHAN BETTS,	JOHN TAYLOR,

WILLIAM PARKER.

II.

The Managers chosen at the first meeting of the Ladies' Society (1836)
were mostly young ladies. These names, as they stand on the list, are:
Mrs. William Belden, Mrs. Harriet (Charles) Gregory, Miss Susan Merwin
(Mrs. George I. Wood), Miss Maria Randle (Mrs. William Ogden), Miss
Mary Cole, Miss Jane Munroe, Miss Jane E. St. John (Mrs. Cyrus Ray-
mond), Miss Susan Hoyt, Miss Susan Comstock, Miss Mary E. Comstock
(Mrs. Lewis Keeler), Miss Mary Middlebrook (Mrs. Harris), Miss Louise
Jessup (Mrs. Thomas B. Gunning).

III.

The following persons were teachers of the Academy for brief periods.
Some of the dates are approximate only:

Xenophen Betts	- - - 1823	William E. Watrous	- -	1842–43
Storrs Hall	- _ - - 1840–41	Odle Close	- - - - -	1843–44
Charles Jones	- - - - 1843–44	James G. Rowland	- -	1846–49
George William Burr	- 1844–45	N. Marvin Belden	- - - —	

IV.

For the Fair in aid of the Church Repairing Fund, held June 26th
and 27th, 1844, at the house of Mr. Nathan Comstock, the following Com-

mittees were appointed some weeks earlier at a meeting of the Ladies' Society. It is safe to believe that a much larger number rendered valuable service at the Fair :

Committee of Superintendence—Miss Dolly Gregory, Mrs. James Betts, Mrs John Smith.

Committee on Ice Cream—Mrs. Charles Marvin, Mrs. George B. Middlebrook, Mrs. George H. Randle.

Committee for Sale of Ice Cream—Misses Mary Ferris and Susan E. Comstock.

To Arrange the Tables—Mrs. C. Marvin, Mrs. G. H. Randle, Mrs. Legrand Comstock ; Misses C. M. Gregory, Clara Willard and Mary Randle.

To Sell Fancy Articles—Miss C. M. Gregory, Miss C. Willard, Mrs. S. Comstock, Miss Martha Keeler, Miss Ann Olmstead and Miss Mary Randle.

To Sell Books—Misses Susan Dudley, Charlotte Betts and Elizab th Willard.

To Attend the Refreshment Tables, were nominated—Mrs. Willard, Mrs. S. P. Randle, Mrs. Maria Ogden; probably many others served.

Door-Keepers—Sylvester D. Willard, Charles M. Gregory.

General Assistants in Preliminary Preparations—Messrs. Legrand Keeler, Legrand Comstock, Lockwood K. Ferris, G. H. Randle and Dr. Sylvester Mead.

Charles St. John, of New York, was very helpful as Auctioneer at the Fair.

V.

The influence of the Church through its Pastor, Dr. Lewis, in favor of education is seen in the four young men (his two sons, also David Belden and Matthew Marvin), whom he is supposed to have fitted for College. Professor Stuart and Rev. William Belden were born during his ministry.

For the last sixty years the influence of the Academy, which, without the Church had not existed, has been so marked, that it is thought best to append a table showing the names of natives and adopted sons of Wilton, who were graduates of College, or entered one of the learned professions, or were authors, editors or teachers ; also of ladies who themselves, or whose husbands, belonged to one of these Classes. The table is necessarily incomplete, but may be helpful to those who celebrate the Centennial of the town, or the second Centennial of the Church:

DAVID LAMBERT (Y. C. 1761).

Dea. MATTHEW MARVIN (Y. C. 1785), died 1842. He was the son of Matthew Marvin and the sixth in descent from Matthew Marvin, one of the first settlers of Norwalk.

Rev. DAVID BELDEN (Y. C. 1785), died 1832. Took orders in the Episcopal Church. Afterwards engaged in farming, and resided in the upper part of Pimpewaug, on the west side of the road, near its junction with the Sugar Hollow turnpike.

Rev. ZECHARIAH LEWIS, and Rev. ISAAC LEWIS, D.D. (twin sons of Rev. Isaac Lewis, D.D.), born January 1st, 1773, graduated at Yale 1794. Useful and honored in many ways. (See Sprague's Annals, vol. 1, p. 666.) Zechariah died in Brooklyn, N. Y., November 14th, 1840 ; Isaac died in New York, September 23d, 1854.

Prof. MOSES STUART (Y. C. 1799), died 1852. See page 76.

Rev. WILLIAM BELDEN (Y. C. 1803), died 1861. Born July 16th, 1781. Son of Azor Belden. From 1812 to 1821 he was Pastor at Greenfield, and Teacher there and afterwards at Fairfield ; also in 1824 to 1843 in New York City. Resided in Brooklyn 1858 to 1861.

BENJAMIN BELDEN, M.D. Son of Azor Belden. Physician, New York City. Still lives.

LEWIS BELDEN, M.D. (Princeton, 1811)., Physician, New York City. Died 1831. Son of Azor Belden.

CHARLES BELDEN M.D. (Princeton, 1812). Son of Azor Belden. Teacher. Died, in New York, "about fifty years ago."

EBENEZER SEELEY, son of Ebenezer (Y. C. 1814). Born April 6th, 1793. Lawyer, many years in New Haven ; afterwards in New York, where he died, January 23d, 1866.

HAWLEY OLMSTEAD, LL.D. (Y. C. 1816), died 1868. See page 52.

ISAAC M. STURGES (Union, 1817), died 1850. Son of Ezekiel Sturges ; lived a farmer at Wilton, and died July 15th, 1850, aged sixty-two years.

DAVID HULL BELDEN, son of Rev. David Belden, lawyer at Newtown, States Attorney, died a few years since.

Dea. CHARLES MARVIN (Y. C. 1823). Son of Dea. Matthew Marvin. Farmer, banker, several times member of the Legislature, and bank commissioner.

Rev. STEPHEN HUBBELL (Y. C. 1826). Son of Nathan and Sarah Hubbell. Ordained at Mount Carmel, May 18th, 1830 ; dismissed 1836. Installed at Wolcottville, February 29th, 1837 ; dismissed September 29th, 1839. Pastor at East Avon, December 31st, 1849, to July 1st, 1853. Pastor at North Stonington, August 17th, 1853, to April 6th, 1869. Pastor at Long Ridge, 1869 to October 28th, 1873. Resides at Mount Carmel, Conn.

Dr. IRA GREGORY. M.D. (Yale Med. School, 1829). Son of Moses and Abigail Gregory. Born January 31st, 1804. Practised medicine at Moriches, Long Island, 1829–1840, and at Norwalk 1840–1872. Deacon in the First Church at Norwalk many years. Died September 2d, 1872.

Dea. JAMES BETTS. See Deacons.

DAVID LAMBERT (Trinity, 1836). Lawyer, editor. Died 1849.

ISAAC M. STURGES. Son of Erastus Sturges. Lawyer; office in Bridgeport.

Rev. Samuel J. M. Merwin (Y. C. 1839). See page 66.

William C. Betts, M.D. (Yale Med. School, 1843). Son of David Betts. Physician in Brooklyn, N. Y. Died 1871.

Rev. Levi Wakeman. Son of William. Not a native, but from early life a resident of Wilton. Learned a trade with Alfred Mallory at Norwalk. Studied in New Haven. Entered the Ministry (Baptist) about thirty years ago. Preached in Stepney, W. Woodstock and New Hartford. Resides in Stamford, Conn.

Lewis R. Hurlbutt, M.D. (Y. C. 1843). Son of John and Elizabeth (Ogden) Hurlbutt. Principal of Bacon Academy, Colchester, 1843–1845; Grammar School, Hartford, 1845–1847. Tutor in Yale College 1847–1850. Physician and surgeon, Stamford, Conn.

Charles Jones (Y. C. 1843). Son of Capt. John Jones. Teacher in Wilton Academy 1843–1844. Member of Legislature of Connecticut 1844. Lawyer, New York City. Residence, Brooklyn.

Rev. John H. Betts (Trinity, 1844). Son of Capt. Ira Betts. Rector in the Episcopal Church in New Hartford and elsewhere.

Dea. Edward Olmstead (Y. C. 1845). See Deacons.

Rev. Samuel G. Willard (Y. C. 1846). Son of Dr. David and Abby (Gregory) Willard. Ordained Pastor at Willimantic, November 8th, 1849 ; dismissed September 8th, 1868. Installed Pastor at Colchester, September 23d, 1868. Member of Y. C. Corporation 1867.

Sylvester D. Willard, M.D. (Albany Med. College, 1847). Son of Dr. David and Abby (Gregory) Willard. Born June 19th, 1825. Secretary of the New York State Medical Society 1857–1865. Practising physician at Albany, N. Y. Surgeon-General 1865. Died April 2d, 1865. Aided to found the Willard Asylum for the Insane at Ovid, N. Y., which was named from him.

Theodore Benjamin. Son of George. Grandson of Dr. Abram Chichester. Born about 1825. Removed to Rochester, N. Y., about 1832. Reported to have entered the Ministry.

John A. Betts, M.D. (Yale Med. School, 1848). Son of David Betts. Brother of Dea. James Betts. Practising physician at Brooklyn, N. Y., where he now resides.

Roger S. Olmstead, M.D. (Yale Med. School, 1849). Son of Hon. Hawley Olmstead. Entered Yale ; studied medicine ; practised in Brooklyn, N. Y. Resides now in Omaha, Neb.

N. Marvin Belden (Trinity, 1849). Son of John A. Belden. Grandson of Rev. David Belden, and of Nathan Marvin. Tutor in Trinity. Resides in Southport.

Rev. Henry L. Hubbell (Y C. 1854). Eldest son of Deacon Wakeman and Julia Lynes Hubbell. Ordained at Amherst, Mass., April 24th, 1861; dismissed April 5th, 1865. Acting-Pastor in Unionville, Conn. Pastor elect Ann Arbor, Michigan, since 1869.

Rev. James W. Hubbell (Y. C. 1857). Son of Deacon W. and Julia L. Hubbell. Ordained at Milford, September 21st, 1864; dismissed June 1st, 1868. Installed June 10th, 1868, College Street Church, New Haven.

Eugene Smith (Y. C. 1859). Son of Matthew and Mary A. (Davenport) Smith. Born in New York City. Resided in Wilton most of the time until after graduation. Lawyer. Resides in New York City.

Coley James. Entered Trinity, 1857. Did not graduate. Received A. M. from Trinity, 1869.

John Henry Hurlbutt. Entered Trinity in 1858, Class of '62, and left June, 1860.

Bela St. John, M.D. Son of Bela St. John. Practised dentistry several years in Danbury; is in gen' ral practice in Wolcottville, Conn.

George Fillow. Son of Seth Fillow. Graduate of State Normal School; teacher in Hartford several years. Residence, Wilton.

Samuel T. Jones. Son of John and Mary (Thorp) Jones. Born December 20th, 1834. Lawyer in New York 1855–1873. Clerk of U. S. District Court. U. S. Commissioner. Died December 24th, 1873.

Samuel H. Olmstead, M.D. (Yale Med. School, 1861). Son of Hawley Olmstead. In practice of medicine and surgeryat Brooklyn, N. Y.

J. Belden Hurlbutt. Son of John Hurlbutt, Jr. Lawyer; office in Norwalk. Acting School Visitor in Wilton.

Rev. John Gaylord Davenport (Williams, 1863). Son of Charles A. and Sarah (Gaylord) Davenport. Pastor, East Bridgeport, Conn. Ordained July 1st, 1868.

Rev. Lewis Gregory (Y. C. 1864). Son of Charles and Harriet (Clark) Gregory. Grandson of Moses. Ordained October 15th, 1868, Pastor, West Amesbury, Mass.; dismissed 1875 to go to Lincoln, Neb., where he is now acting-Pastor.

Clarence L. Westcott (Y. C. 1864). Son of George B. and Arethusa (Lincoln) Westcott. Lawyer, New York City.

Charles F. Morgan, M.D. (Y. C. Med. School, 1866). Son of Charles A. and Electa B. Morgan. Physician in practice at Norwalk.

Samuel Keeler (Y. C. 1867). Son of Legrand W. and Catharine (Lockwood) Keeler. Lawyer, New York City.

Strong Comstock (Y. C. 1867). Son of Capt. James and Harriet (Betts) Comstock. Teacher, Walton, N. Y.

Gordon Hall, A.B. (Amherst, about 1869). Son of Rev. Gordon Hall, D.D. Banker, Northampton, Mass.

Daniel Davenport (Y. C. 1873). Son of Judge George A. and Mary (Sturges) Davenport. Lawyer, Bridgeport.

Timothy Davenport (Y. C. 1875). Brother of Daniel. Law student.

Benjamin Davenport. Brother of preceding, and member for a time of Class of 1875, Y. C. Lawyer, Washington, D. C.

DAVID R. LAMBERT.   Son of Samuel Lambert, and member for a time of Class of 1875, Y. C. Residence, Wilton.

SAMUEL E. MORGAN, M.D. (Yale Col. Med. School, 1875). Son of Charles A. and Electa B. Morgan. Residence, Wilton.

CHARLES GILBERT (W. C. 1876). Son of Dea. Benajah and Fanny (Keeler) Gilbert.

I. CHAUNCEY STURGES (graduated at Berkley Div. School, Middletown, 1876). Son of J. Randall Sturges. Residence, Kent, Conn.

FREDERIC D. BENEDICT (two years at Y. C. in Class of 1867 ; Danville Theo. Sem., Kentucky). Son of I. Newton and Emily (Keeler) Benedict.

———

SUSAN COMSTOCK (Mrs. Requa), d. Strong. Missionary of Am. Board in 1822 to Osage Indians. Married Rev. William C. Requa.

ANN HUBBELL (Mrs. Dr. Nash), d. Nathan Hubbell. Married Mr. Burr, of Fairfield, who died early. One son, George William Burr, member for a time of the Class of 1846 Y. C. ; afterwards a lawyer in New York, who died about 1860. Married Dr. William B. Nash, Bridgeport, who died in 1873. Resides in New Haven.

JANE BELDEN (Mrs. Booth), d. Rev. David Belden. Married Reuben Booth (Y. C. 1816), lawyer, Lieut.-Gov. Connecticut. Resided in Danbury. Died 1844.

ABBY GREGORY (Mrs. Dr. Willard), d. Moses. Born April 20th, 1797. Married Dr. David Willard, December 22d, 1818. Died January 3d, 1857.

HENRIETTA BELDEN (Mrs. Dr. Stone), d. Col. William and Mrs. Becca Belden. Married Dr. Stone and went South. Both died early.

MARIA HUBBELL (Mrs. Dr. Lewis), d. Nathan Hubbell. Married Dr. Lewis, of Brockport, N. Y.

HARRIET CANNON (Mrs. Todd), d. George Cannon. Married about 1834 Rev. Charles Todd, Rector of the Episcopal Church in Wilton. She died in Huntington, Conn., 1849.

ESTHER M. TAYLOR, d. Levi Taylor. About 1838 married Dr. Ambrose L. White, surgeon, U. S. A. Died 1876.

LOUISA JESSUP (Mrs. Gunning), d. William and Nancy (Odell) Jessup. Graduate of Rutgers Institute ; teacher in New York. Married about 1844 Dr. Thomas B. Gunning, dental surgeon, New York.

ELIZABETH JESSUP (Mrs Reed), d. William. Married James Reed, editor of the Norwalk *Gazette*, and now, for many years, editor of the Ashtabula *Telegraph*, Ohio.

EMILY JESSUP, d. William. Graduate of Mt. Holyoke ; was several years assistant teacher there, and now occupies the position of first assistant in the Western Female Seminary, Oxford, Ohio.

CHARLOTTE BETTS (Mrs. Barnum), sister Dea. James Betts. Teacher. Married Rev. Samuel W. Barnum (Y. C. 1841), who was ordained January 25th, 1853. Pastor, Massachusetts, to 1862. Editor "Abridgement Smith's Bible Dictionary," and other works. Residence, New Haven.

MARY RANDLE (Mrs. Willard), d. Samuel P. and Sally (Hyatt) Randle. Born June 8th, 1821. Studied at Wilton Academy and Utica (N. Y.) Female Seminary. Married Rev. S. G. Willard, November 14th, 1849. Died at Willimantic, May 15th, 1853.

CLARA A. WILLARD, d. Dr. David W. Born February 4th, 1823. Studied in Wilton and Bridgeport. Teacher of private and family school twenty years, or more, in Wilton. Author of "Nellie Greyson," "Fifty Years Ago," and other works. Died at Norwalk, February 15th, 1876.

ELIZABETH WILLARD (Mrs. L. J. Curtis), d. Dr. David W. Married, April 2d, 1850, James G. Rowland (Y. C. 1846), who opened a family school for boys in Kent, and died August 20th, 1853. Mrs. B. continued the school, and taught till 1864. October 20th, 1864, she married Lewis J. Curtis, of Norwalk.

MARY WILLARD (Mrs. Salmon C. Gillett), d. Dr. David W. Studied in New Haven. Teacher for years. Residence, Colchester, Ct.

SUSAN WILLARD (Mrs. Mix), d. Dr. David W. Taught for a time. May 1st, 1860, married Rev. Eldridge Mix (Williams College, 1854). He was assistant to the Rev. Dr. Hastings (New York) 1860–61; Pastor in Burlington, Vt., 1862 to August 20th, 1867 ; Pastor First Church in Orange, N. J., 1867.

ELIZABETH MIDDLEBROOK (Mrs. Hill), d. Col. George M. Married, 1856, John Hill, M.D., for some years physician and surgeon in Brooklyn, N. Y.; now in South Norwalk.

LUCRETIA MIDDLEBROOK (Mrs. Brown), d. Col. George M. Married Augustus Brown, lawyer, Ballston, N. Y. Mr. and Mrs. Brown died early.

GERTRUDE MIDDLEBROOK (Mrs. Turner), d. Col. George M. Married J. Edward Turner, M.D., the founder and first Superintendent of the Binghamton Asylum for Inebriates. They reside in Wilton.

HARRIET FITCH (Mrs. Gregory), d. J. Platt Fitch. Married Rev. Abel Ogden (Trinity, 1842), some time Rector of St. Matthew's Church, Wilton, who died 1854; married, second time, to Rev. Luther Gregory, Rector of St. Paul's Church, Huntington, who died about 1863.

MARY W. GREGORY (Mrs. Hubbell), d. Charles. Married Rev. James W. Hubbell, A.D. 1861. Residence, New Haven.

ALICE WESTCOTT (Mrs. J. G. Davenport), d. George B. Married Rev. John G. Davenport, Bridgeport.

LOUISA RANDLE, daughter George H. and Caroline (Lounsbury) Randle. Lady Principal, Seminary, Penn Yan, New York.

HELEN RANDLE (Mrs. Barnum), d. George. H. Graduate of State Normal School. Married Rev. Henry S. Barnum (Y. C. 1862) March 10th, 1869. Mr. Barnum is in the service of the American Board. They are stationed at Van, Eastern Turkey.

SARAH RANDLE (Mrs. Steele), d. George H. Married, August 2d, 1865, to Rev. John B. Steele, who was ordained Aug. 16th, 1865, preached several years in Western New York, and died November 29th, 1873, aged thirty-eight years, at Middlebury, Vt., where she resides.

JANET HOLMES (Mrs. Paine), d. George Holmes. Married Levi L. Paine, D.D. (Y. C. 1856), Professor of Ecclesiastical History, Theol. Sem., Bangor, Me.

MARY A. DAVENPORT (Mrs. White), d. George A. Married Dr. Charles B. White, surgeon, U.S.A., son of Dr. Ambrose L. White, and grandson of Levi Taylor.

MARTHA BELDEN (Mrs. Warren), d. John A. Married, A.D. 1869, Dr. Warren, of Norwich, Conn., who died some years ago.

CLARINA STURGES, d. Charles. Graduate Mt. Holyoke. Married. Resides in Brookfield, Conn.

JOSEPHINE STURGES, d. Charles. Graduate Mt. Holyoke. Married O. A. G. Todd, lawyer, Danbury.

ARTEMESIA STURGES, d. Charles. Student for a while at Mt. Holyoke. Teacher of music. Married.

JANE D. MIDDLEBROOK (Mrs. Foote), d. George B. Married Joseph F. Foote, lawyer, Norwalk.

ELIZABETH MIDDLEBROOK (Mrs. Barber), d. George B. A.D. 1870, married James W. Barber, M.D., Norwalk.

FRANCESCA BETTS (Mrs. Nesbit), d. John C. Married Rev. Alexander Nesbit (graduate of N. Y. Col.), Pastor of the Presbyterian Church, Tremont, N. Y., who died in 1875.

LETTERS

IN REPLY TO INVITATIONS OF THE COMMITTEE.

LETTER FROM DR. G. HALL.

TO THE CONGREGATIONAL CHURCH IN WILTON:

BELOVED—Although it is nearly a quarter of a century since my Pastoral connection with you was severed, I still retain a lively, affectionate interest in the Church of my first love.

It is a matter of sore regret that I could not be present at the late gathering, commemorative of the one hundred and fiftieth year of your existence as an organization; but a combination of circumstances seemed to render it impracticable.

The four men who were, perhaps, more influential than any others in securing my settlement in Wilton, about twenty-eight years ago, still survive, and participated in your recent festivities.

These friends, and indeed all who counselled with me respecting my call to your parish, were truthful and thoroughly honest in their representations—as is not always the case when a new Pastor is sought. They reported to me the exact state of feeling, how many voted for me, and how many declined; and their prophecy was, that in six months those very ones who took no part in calling me would be among my firmest friends. This proved true. I found none but friends in the Church and parish If, during my stay among you, any word was spoken or any act done, out of unkind intent towards me, it never came to my knowledge.

The contract under which I settled in Wilton was more than fulfilled. Liberality towards me increased each succeeding year of my Pastorate among you.

In one respect particularly, as I look back, I admire the kindness and forbearance of the long-suffering people. When I recollect that my sermons at times exceeded an hour in length, and that the hearers bore it good-naturedly, I think they must have had great deference to the "everlasting" Gospel and great tenderness for the young man who spread his matter over such a superficial area. But I suppose they had hope of my improvement in this respect, as venerable ministerial brethren had for my ortho-doxy when some of the "new school kinks" should be taken out of me.

I could fill many pages with reminiscences of my short ministry in your town. I remember some marked characters with whom I had to do. I have my associations with visits and hospitality and meetings in Pimpewaug and Kent, and Bald Hill and Belden's Hill, and Chicken street and Nod, &c. I recall faithful workers—men and women—in these various districts who were an encouragement and a help. We were permitted to rejoice together over many souls won to the Kingdom of Christ. These fellow-workers, many of them, have gone to their reward.

Removal from my Wilton charge was effected without losing their confidence or good will. So that the way has been open for visiting my old parish with delight. It has been my privilege to preach at the settlement of two Pastors who succeeded me, and I have rejoiced in the good and able men whom you have had for your ministers. May the Lord continue such in a long succession to this ancient and honored Church, and maintain a growing, active, faithful membership of men and women and children, and send forth, as He has in years past, many to preach the Gospel and honor the Christian name in various walks of life! The Lord bless thee and thy helpers, and make thee a praise and an excellency from generation to generation.

Yours, in abiding affection,

GORDON HALL.

Northampton, Mass., July 5th, 1876.

———*cu.*———

ABSTRACT OF LETTER RECEIVED FROM REV. S. R. DIMOCK.

CENTRAL CITY, Col., }
July 10th, 1876. }

DEAR FRIEND OLMSTEAD: Your letter found me on the top of the Rocky Moun-tains, whither, perhaps the Lord hath sent me up to die. In my school-boy days I read of these mountains, but never dreamed they were to be my future home. Though your letter came too late for the grand celebration, yet it made no difference, for the distance and expense would have prevented my attendance. Yet how gladly would I have been with you, for I dearly love that ancient Church and the dear people to whom I ministered so pleasantly for a year and a half. Though there is little prospect of it at present, I still cherish the hope of visiting you again before I die.

* * * * * * * * * * *

I wish you in some way to assure the people that my affection for them has grown stronger and stronger as the years have glided away. And now that the cloud of sor-row has lifted in a measure, I find the hope reviving that I may, ere long, visit the scenes of happy memory, and express in person to my former people my continued con-fidence and love. My daughter also (now sixteen) has a strong desire to visit the old parsonage where she was born, and form the acquaintance of her father's friends whom she was too young to remember.

Most truly yours,

S. R. DIMOCK.

LETTER FROM REV. LEWIS GREGORY.

LINCOLN, Nebraska,
June 17, 1876

MR. EDWARD OLMSTEAD:

DEAR FRIEND—In a letter received from Rev. S. R. Dimock, my predecessor in the Church here and now of Central City, Colorado, he said: "Little did I think, when preaching in Wilton fifteen years ago, of going out into the Great American Desert to prepare the way for one of the boys of my congregation." But so it was to be. And from the Desert, now "blossoming as the rose," I send back to the dear mother Church and her sons and daughters gathered to observe her birth-day, the heartiest greetings. Besides the attachment one always feels for the home of his childhood, I love the Church as the birth-place and home of my soul. It has always seemed to me that the beauty of its landscape, the excellence of its Academy, the intelligence of its ladies, and the many quaint people to be found among its inhabitants, give Wilton a peculiar charm. Though fifteen hundred miles of land separate us, I assure you my heart is with you in the commemoration of the dear old Church's anniversary. It may interest some of my old school-mates to know that I am trying to build up the cause of Education and Religion in this young State, and have daily reason to thank God for His blessing upon my labors, and the early Wilton training which fitted me for helping to lay the foundations in this new country.

Our city already numbers eight thousand people, and is rapidly growing. Outside of the University towns you could hardly find in the East as large a proportion of liberally educated people as here

Give my love to all enquiring friends, and believe me,

Ever yours,

LEWIS GREGORY.

———:o:———

LETTER FROM REV. MR. HARVEY.

[IN reply to a letter of inquiry, in which the seven questions were for convenience numbered, this letter was received from the Rev. Mr. Harvey. His answer follows the order of the questions It was written with no thought of its being published, or used in its present form; but it was so highly prized by those to whom it was read, that the author, with some reluctance, consents that his friends use it as they think best.   S. G. W.]

BROADWAY, N Y.,
June 16th, 1876.

REV. S. G. WILLARD:

DEAR BROTHER—In answer to yours of the 13th, I send the following :

1. I was born at Jamestown, Chatauqua County, New York.

2. April 15th, 1825— new style.

3. I am the son of Charles R. Harvey,

which was the son of Rufus   "
which was the son of Jonathan   "
which was the son of William   "
which was the son of Thomas   "
which was the son of William   "

who emigrated to this country from England, and bought what is now the town of Taunton, Mass, from the Indians for a peck of beans.

He was the great-grandson of Turner Harvey—a noted archer and warrior, the mightiest man with his bow in all England. At his death there was no man in England who could spring his bow. He was born about 1500.

My mother's name was Olive Willard I am proud of my connection with the Willard family. Perhaps you may not be ashamed to acknowledge me as your thirty-ninth cousin, especially as I am not a Presidential candidate.

4. Graduated in 1844 at the University of the City of New York.

5. Imbibed a limited amount of theology at the Union Theological Seminary in this City.

6. My wife's father's name was Edward Lewis. Her mother's name was Cynthia Gildersleeve, of Portland, Conn. My wife is an excellent woman.

7. "Several other things" must be imagined. My life has been uneventful, except four children. I never was burned at the stake, though the "steak" has been too often burned for me.

I do not receive a pension for my services in the late war, nor do I suppose that I have any particular claim upon the admiration and gratitude of the latest posterity. Without official title or honor I wearily toil in the dusty highways of life, and am so deaf that I can't hear a man when he asks me for money

I should be very happy to attend the Wilton Centennial, but poverty clothes me with seedy babiliments, and makes me anxious to save my last dollar to buy your "Historical Address" I hope, as I believe, that I shall not be missed. With many thanks for your kindness, I remain

Yours truly,

WHEELOCK NYE HARVEY.